THE MISTRESS, THE MONSTER AND THE MARQUESS

AMELIA SHAW

TAMSIN BAKER

Lina hadn't fed in weeks and was getting to the point where she needed blood. With a jaded eye she leaned against the pillar in her main sitting room, simply observing the men in front of her. Hopefully there would be someone looking for trouble—it would give her an excuse to drain them dry. Being over four hundred years old, her blood needs were minimal. Which meant she could wait for the perfect smell, the exact perfumed skin she desired to entice her to feed. Tonight, wouldn't be one of those such moments, it seemed.

A high-pitched squeal from the back corner caught her attention.

She moved there, swift as lightning, before another sound could be made. "Take your hands off her, now." She gripped the wrist of the slovenly dressed gentleman who was sliding his hand up the inside of Marie's thigh and tried to rein her temper in. It wouldn't be good business to harm him in front of everyone. Especially as she wanted to maintain her reputation of being a hospitable hostess.

However, Lina despised the gentlemen that came into her expensive, well-run brothel and treated her girls like common dock tarts. They may be whores in a whorehouse, but they were selling their wares and craft, and deserved to be chosen respectfully and then taken to a private room.

The man, whom she knew to be drunk and well into his late forties, turned up his lip. "I'm paying for her. I'll do whatever I like."

Lina smiled, her fangs tingling in her gum line and threatening to reveal themselves. Only years of focus and training stopped them from sliding out of her mouth with menace. She didn't want to have to move towns again. There were rules about vampires exposing themselves, after all. "Sir, after you pay, you may take Marie to her room. But know this, I do not allow my girls to be hurt."

Lina used a small amount of her real strength to squeeze the man's wrist bones together. They made a sickening crunch which was very satisfying and made her crave more. *How good would it feel to break his legs?* she mused.

He groaned and nodded as he removed his other hand from Marie's thigh.

Marie stood awkwardly and flicked her skirts down with practiced ease. She'd been born a noble lady but had since fallen on hard times.

Lina felt sorry for the gentle, well-mannered soul and tried to avoid giving her to men like him. "Actually," she said, her decision made. *This man will not have Marie.* "Jane?" Lina turned and snapped her fingers, calling out to her most experienced whore.

Jane was as tough as nails and could withstand even their roughest clientele, though Lina promised her a rescue whenever needed. Jane pressed her full breasts that were barely covered by her chemise, into the gentleman's side. "This way, sir," she said batting her eyelashes. "You'll *love* my room."

The man looked back at Marie's beautiful face, then down at Jane's with a grimace.

When compared to slender and young Marie, Jane was certainly plain and definitely older, but she was buxom and what she lacked in youth and beauty she made up for with skill and enthusiasm. She was reliable and ensured each client left satisfied with their visit.

Lina smiled without humor, knowing exactly what the man was

about to say. She wasn't a mind reader like the others of her brethren, but she had empathy and had been reading facial expressions, body language, and scent cues for centuries. "I know you want Marie, sir, but these are my premises, and you *will* abide the mistress of the house. I can promise you; Jane will not disappoint."

Jane dropped a hand to the man's crotch and began to rub him while she whispered promises of pleasure into his ear.

They were gone in mere moments.

Lina inhaled deeply, relieved, and found her nose filled with the most incredible of aromas. It was akin to a mixture of honey and ambrosia, the nectar of the gods. It looked like she wouldn't have to make do with just anyone's blood tonight. Her ideal prey had arrived. She turned slowly, forcing herself to enjoy the hunt, to anticipate and savor the first time she looked upon him—whoever he may be.

And there he was. Her prey was beautiful, but then, they always were. Perhaps not to everyone's taste, but always to hers. Though this one in particular was tall, broad, and handsome—a man who could easily steal the heart of anyone. He smelled simply divine, his warm blood pumping along his veins in time with his heart, an intoxicating rhythm that called to her as strongly and surely as any siren song. *Yes, he will do just fine.* "Can I help you gentlemen?"

There were four men in total in their company, all about thirty years of age. The other three were all red faced and overweight, with long foppish hair that reached to their shoulders.

Lina placed her hands on her hips and glanced up from under her long, dark lashes as she sashayed towards them. People considered her beautiful, she knew that without question. Preserved at a perfect age for both sexual appeal and beauty, her maker had been very clever, and she thanked him for the precious gift of immortality often.

Her gentleman stood in front of the assembled group and spoke for them all.

"We heard you were the best madam in all of London. My friends would like a woman each, please," he said as he bowed to her with an almost imperceptible shudder, the scent of his arousal rolling off him in waves.

Her body quickened in response, and she salivated. "Of course, gentlemen. Please, come in, and find a girl you like. She will then escort you to her room." Lina indicated the women around the room and smiled invitingly at her newest patrons.

She ran a clean and upper-class brothel. Each girl had her own room, her own sheets, her own toys, and Lina guaranteed their safety. She knew how hard it was to make a livelihood as a single female and could sympathize with every one of her girls. She couldn't get them out of this life because she needed to also make a living too, but she could keep them safe and in enough coin to live comfortably. They only needed to whisper her name and she would be there.

As a vampire her hearing was exceptional, her strength unsurpassed by any human living or dead. No man hurt one of her girls and got away unscathed. She believed firmly that unsavory behavior should be rewarded with an equally adequate deterrent.

Each of the men surrounding her prey left him and found a girl. None of them felt dangerous. They just reeked of arousal and alcohol, which was a good combination for an easy night.

Her man remained standing in the center of the room, watching her with a lustful gaze.

"Do none of my girls catch your eye, sir?" she asked, twirling a lock of her long red hair tantalizingly around a slender finger.

The gentleman looked straight at her, his shoulders tall and proud.

She held his gaze, admiring his green eyes—the unique and beautiful way in which they were smattered with flecks of intriguing yellow.

"No, thank you. I am here to make sure everyone gets home safely."

Lina inhaled sharply, her stomach tightening with need. His voice was deep and soothing, and he didn't desire any of her girls, which pleased her immensely. No gentleman had ever said no to her before, and so she assumed that if she offered herself, now, she would not be refused. He was beyond handsome; in fact, his face was remarkably beautiful, like an angel carved in stone by a great artist. And his scent intoxicated her more with every breath she drew. Sweet, yet strong, and deliciously forbidden.

Surprised by the strength of her reaction, Lina tried to hold her breath, but to no avail. Her body was still responding with more than just blood hunger. She had not lusted after a human physically in a very long time and had quite truthfully forgotten what it felt like.

Usually when she fed she would wait until her chosen prey had fallen asleep with one of her girls, then she would take the blood she needed. They were none the wiser and she was left satisfied. This one seemed special somehow, though… and she hadn't fucked a human in so long. *Perhaps it's time once again?*

She stepped closer to him and spoke directly into his ear. "I am clean, though I can't guarantee your safety. Would you like to spend some quality time with me tonight?"

The scent of his lust spiked at her suggestion, but Lina also sensed shock.

"Thank you, but no," he answered formally with a tight throat.

A real gentleman, how unusual. Undeterred, Lina drew back and smiled her most seductive smile. "Wait until all of your friends are settled and come find me. I have something I would like to show you."

The man's eyes widened again and his nostrils flared. He was picking up on her scent, which was always a positive sign.

Lina needed blood, but she was also uncharacteristically aroused. This man would be perfect for satisfying *both* her cravings. She flicked her magnificent red hair and walked across the room to her only male servant, swinging her hips in a provocative way as she went. "Look after everything for me, will you dear? But do call if you need me, I won't be far away."

Charles nodded; he'd witnessed her strength before and wouldn't hesitate to call for her.

Lina's gentleman strode up to her unexpectedly and bowed with an exaggerated flourish she didn't deserve given her station as the madam of a brothel. "Is there somewhere that I might wait for my friends? Somewhere more private, perhaps?" he asked hopefully, gesturing to the heavy petting and drinking going on around them.

"Of course, sir." Lina inclined her head, took his arm in the polite fashion, and guided him along the short hallway. Her belly trembled with nerves, the kind she hadn't experienced in decades. The feeling was as unusual as it was welcome and refreshing. When they reached the door to her underground room, she pressed her eternally youthful and supple body into his, pushing him into the wall.

He was solid and warm, a perfect combination.

"I know you want me, my lord, there is no need to fight it." Lina reached up and ran the backs of her nails gently down his smooth face as she swayed her hips against his hardening cock. Her own body responded to his obvious arousal, heating, and preparing itself to take him. "I will take you out of yourself and give you pleasure the likes of which you have never felt." She leaned forward and nipped at his earlobe, using her tongue to taste the saltiness of his skin. "You need only give me the chance to show you."

Lina felt the shiver that went through her prey and was surprised by the intense rush of need she felt for him. She saw human men as her sustenance and livelihood, and usually no more. Yet, on this occasion, she was amazed at how much she was earnestly looking forward to pleasuring this one.

The gentleman drew a steady breath and used his hands to slowly ease her back, looking her directly in the eyes once again. He seemed hesitant but determined to follow through with his chosen path. "If it pleases you, my lady, I have reconsidered and would like to take you up on your generous offer." He trembled as he spoke, his natural instincts serving him well. He was afraid and yet so inexorably tempted by what she promised that he couldn't resist.

Lina smiled at her beautiful prey, most pleased. She was no lady. Certainly not the sort he was used to dealing with anyway. "This way, my lord."

Lina unlocked the door that led to her underground bedroom, her private chambers, her daytime resting place, and her playroom for the vampiric men she took to her bed. She began to descend the steps, feeling his anxiety escalate as they made their way down. By the fifty-seventh step, the last one, his fear thickened the air like a pungent smell.

"Where are we?" he asked.

"My dungeon." Lina felt her prey's flicker of arousal, beating against the fear still surrounding him like a dark cloud.

"Have I been bad, my lady?"

His teasing tone lit a long dead fire in her belly. It had been too long since she had spoken to a human like this.

CHAPTER

TWO

Lina's pussy was wet and aching for him already. But the question remained... play with him? Or just fuck him? She watched his face as he glanced around the well-lit room.

Fascination and fear warred for dominance over his expression as he took in the chamber's beauty.

"Do you have a lot of responsibility, my lord?" Lina circled her prey and pulled his tailored jacket down and off his shoulders, draping it on a nearby wall hook.

He didn't even put up a token resistance, increasing his appeal to her.

No weak lord this one. He wants to play!

"Yes, I do my lady. Why do you ask?"

"It's Lina," she crooned, before she began unbuttoning his shirt. Dropping her eyes to her hands, she felt marginally embarrassed that she had told him her name so easily; but with what she had in mind for him? *My lady* would just not do.

"Benedict." he offered.

Lina looked up at his charming face and her breath caught in her throat. His smile was exceptional. Human beauty, for the most part, was fleeting and of no real interest to her, but this one was simply remarkable. With a square and masculine jaw, lovely, thick short-cropped brown hair, and the smoothest, cleanest skin—he was simply divine.

His shirt dropped to the floor, and she sighed as she circled him again. He had the body of a hard-working laborer, not a lay-about English lord, that much was evident. He was thickly muscled and had a gorgeous golden-brown sun-kissed complexion. She missed these sorts of men. Most of the gentlemen of the London ton were white, slender, and soft like reeds. *Horrible really.*

Benedict stood as still as a statue, neither touching her nor moving. Perfectly submissive.

"Benedict, I would like you to surrender yourself to me. Let me use you as I wish, trust me implicitly. And I will make all of your responsibilities and worries melt away."

Benedict chuckled as he looked around her room at the impressive array of chains, riding crops, whips, and various lengths of rope. He obviously knew what she was suggesting as the scent of his arousal climbed even higher.

Lina's fangs extended with longing. He smelled too good to be true. "You wish to tie me up, Lina?"

Lina moved surreptitiously around behind him and concentrated on getting her fangs to retract. She didn't want them out at the moment and hadn't had a problem with control in a *very* long time. His delectable appeal was testing her. She slid her hands around his waist to unfasten his breeches. "Yes, I do. I will whip you and suck you. Then, if you are lucky? I will fuck you."

Her living statue trembled as her words whispered across his hot skin. His hands clenching into fists at his sides, but he still didn't move an inch.

"Step out of your breeches, my pet," she commanded as she pushed his breeches down for him. A groan slipped from her lips when she felt his huge cock swing free and brush against her arm. She had felt it lurking beneath the layers of his clothing, straining for freedom, but had never imagined it would be so beautiful. The shaft was big and thick, the head broad and pink with blood.

Another gush of fluid lubricated her wanton pussy. There really wasn't any choice. She definitely had to fuck him. Focusing on pushing her hunger for Benedict's blood down to a less rampant level, she stalled for time. She wanted to play with her prey for a little while before giving into the ultimate temptation. "Walk over to the wooden step to your left."

Benedict turned his head and located the piece of equipment she was talking about.

Lina sensed his fear inch up a notch, but he did as he was told. Lina watched him move, feeling his emotions flow through her as though they were her own. He was naturally confident, strong, and sure of himself. She would make him submit to her and when he did, he would find the greatest of pleasures in it.

"Now, lay across the bench and reach over as far down as you can."

His eyes flashed a little, mutiny gathering in those beautiful yellow flecks. "Lina, I'm not going to..."

"You will do as I tell you to, Benedict." She placed a soft blanket over the wood to protect his pelvis, then she pointed at the bench expectantly. She could make him, she was far stronger, but this type of pleasure had to be accepted willingly. There simply was no other way.

"Will you hurt me?" he asked hesitantly.

She flashed him a smile no one had ever managed to resist. "Yes, but I will not *harm* you. If you yell stop, I'll stop. You have my word."

His eyes narrowed as he replayed her words over in his mind, clearly weighing up his limited options.

She held his gaze, then pointed again, a single brow raised.

He sighed then, but laid over the wood, his buttocks high, round, and delightfully firm.

Lina groaned at the sight. *What a magnificent specimen of a human male.* She knelt on the floor quickly to secure his ankles and wrists to the four separate legs of the bench, spreading him wide as she did so. Lina then stood and removed the annoying barriers of her dress, chemise, and shoes. Clad only in her garter belt and silk stockings, she pressed herself against Benedict's ass, her wet pussy aching for relief against the need clawing at her.

"Fuck... Lina!" Benedict struggled against his bonds, but they were far too strong for a mere human to break free from.

"Such a nice ass you have, Benedict, and not a single mark on it. Would you like me to spank you?"

He was silent as she reached between his legs and cupped his warm and heavy sac.

"Perhaps," he finally answered.

The light, teasing tone of his response made her smile. She loved his cheekiness. With unparalleled control, she swung her arm and spanked him: twice on the left cheek and four times on the right.

He cried out at the last touch.

She leaned forward to kiss his rosy, pink skin. "Did you like that, my pet?" She ran her hands down the back of his powerful thighs and back up his ass once again.

"I'm not quite sure."

Lina smiled again. An honest response. *How pleasantly unusual.*

"I need something more."

Using her vampiric speed, Lina chose a riding crop from the wall and was back before Benedict realized she had moved at all. "I think you are a good man, Benedict, but also a very bad boy. Shall I use my riding crop on you?"

She ran the leather up and down his spine, his arousal appeared to lessen with the increase of fear. So, Lina moved away and swung the crop lightly, barely connecting with his flesh.

He yelped a little but tilted his pelvis up for more.

She swung the crop harder, catching the soft flesh of his upper thigh, just under his ass.

He groaned this time.

Promising. "I need to hear it, pet. Tell me."

"Yes. More," he begged.

She swung the crop repeatedly, measuring her strength carefully and only landing the leather on the softest parts of her new lover.

She stopped when his skin began to glow red, and ran her cool, bare hands gently over his ass. "Are you okay, my pet?"

He nodded, sweat gathering on his skin, but said nothing.

Lina reached between his legs and found his cock still hard, his balls tight. She sucked her middle finger into her mouth, coating it with copious saliva. Then she slid the wet finger into his tight ass at the same time she used her other hand to reach around and firmly grab his cock.

"What? No..." Benedict gasped, struggling at the foreign invasion. Mere moments later he moaned as she crooked her finger with practiced ease and hit all a man's known sweet spots.

"Better?" she purred.

He moaned again, his cock growing even harder, straining beneath its thin film of fine skin.

So beautiful. "Tell me, pet, is this better?"

"Yes... *Oh, God...* fuck!" His words trailed off as he groaned in pleasure.

Lina stilled her hands with a lewd smile on her lips. Should she make him come like this, and then wait for him to become hard again?

"Stop Lina, please, I want your pussy," said Benedict, breaking into her thoughts.

Lina scowled down at the man trying to tell her what to do, before she slowly removed her fingers.

He moaned in desperation. He was too close; he would never last for her.

Lina bent down and untied his wrists and ankles.

He straightened slowly, his eyes a glazed-over mess of colors.

"You'll never please me for long enough," she stated in a matter-of-fact tone. "You'll be gone in moments."

His eyes cleared of their fogginess, and he smiled with a confidence she couldn't help but admire. "I believe you are wrong about me, Lina. I have staying power."

His cocky words amused her, then he surprised her when he picked her up by the waist and turned with her, sitting her on the blanket he had just previously occupied. Her prey stepped between her thighs and pressed his hard cock to her sopping wet entrance.

"Do you want this?" he asked.

Wetness dripped down her thighs and a deep ache ate away at her core. She wanted him so badly, it was incredible. How could a mere human make her want him so much? She frowned at him, determined to remain in control and maintain her position of dominance during their tryst. "Use your mouth on me," she ordered, her expression stern.

Benedict's eyes grew wide, then even more interestingly, a fire of renewed heat lit their depths.

A man who wants to lick my cunt? Perfect!

"Yes, I will." He dropped to his knees and pushed open her legs with his strong hands.

Lina leaned back, her supernatural strength making it easy to keep her balance.

He held her fast, his fingers digging into her thighs as he leaned forward and began to lick her swollen clit.

An unexpected scream tore from her throat, shocking her, and she grabbed at Benedict's head in dire need.

He was ruthless as he pleasured her, suckling the aroused flesh over and over, before running his tongue up and down her slit, lapping at the sweet juices seeping from her very core.

Her orgasm was fast approaching, but she needed blood tonight. It could not be delayed. "Fuck me, pet," she commanded urgently. "Fuck me now like your life depends on it."

Benedict moved so fast, even Lina was shocked. He grabbed her ass with both hands, lined up his cockhead, and plunged in to the hilt.

"*Fuck!*" Lina threw back her head and screamed again as her empty, and needy body was filled by the hot, powerful man thundering between her thighs.

Benedict didn't wait a single moment, he just moved right back and thrust in to the hilt again, impaling her mercilessly.

She cried out again, the angle perfect to rouse the simmering fire and building hunger of her body.

Over and over again he fucked her deep, using his firm grip on her ass to pull her forward and onto him.

Lina wrapped her stocking-covered legs around his back and laced her arms around his neck. She kissed the side of his throat, tasting the saltiness of his skin as her belly coiled in anticipation. Her orgasm was set to reach dizzying heights. Her pussy tightened and then her head exploded in an array of stars. She opened her mouth and felt her fangs descend. Screaming out as her orgasm rippled through her, her cunt squeezed around Benedict's cock.

Her prey thrust hard into her and cried out, his body pulsating inside her pussy as his orgasm gripped him, their releases perfectly synchronized.

Lina moaned and sunk her fangs into his skin. Sweet, delicious, and intoxicating blood filled her mouth, and she closed her eyes, swallowing mouthfuls of his crimson essence as his hot seed flooded her, completing her, and nourishing her.

CHAPTER

THREE

Benedict came back to his body very slowly, as if awakening from a dream. He had never had an orgasm last that long or feel so intense. It felt like he'd actually passed out for a moment when it reached its crescendo. Whores were not his first choice for sexual pleasure; he had a fulltime mistress for that. He normally detested the cold comfort, and the empty feelings that came with these sorts of couplings.

But if this time was anything to go by, he may have just changed his mind. This dalliance with Lina had been the strangest fuck of his life, but also the most physically satisfying. It was crazy, but he wanted more.

He gazed down at Lina; her eyes were closed in bliss, her head resting against his shoulder. Her cunt was still clamped tightly around him, which felt so perfect he didn't even have the words to truly describe it. He never wanted to leave the scrumptious wet warmth of her body.

Then he focused on her mouth, and the unmistakable trail of red blood on her lower lip and chin. *What the hell?*

The sight of his own blood jogged his memory, reminding him of the flashes of dreams he had seen. As he had reached orgasm, what he could only guess was a vision had shown him an old man with long, white hair. He had heard him speak and felt him as if he were real. It was without doubt the strangest thing he had ever experienced, this fuck included.

Benedict shifted his feet, thinking quickly. He had heard the legends of course, tales of creatures that required blood to survive the way humans needed food. He wiggled his toes and mentally checked his health internally. He seemed fine. She hadn't harmed him, just as she said she wouldn't.

Cock completely flaccid now, he reluctantly withdrew from her.

In response, she unwrapped her lithe body from his and jumped down from her sex perch.

His lover, a woman that he believed was a genuine vampire, walked away and stepped back into her gown with grace. She was the singularly most beautiful woman he had ever seen. Her skin was so smooth it looked like thick, fresh cream and glowed with good health —his good health probably. In fact, she was looking more and more radiant by the minute.

Stepping back into his breeches, he pulled them back up over his lower body and buttoned himself up. He didn't offer to pay her, since she had clearly taken as much as he'd given.

Lina turned to him, her blue eyes shining as she watched him sharply.

"Thank you, Benedict. You may leave whenever you like."

He stilled. *Was she dismissing him?* Disappointment hit him hard, followed by a heavy dose of anger. He did not enjoy the feeling of being used and tossed aside.

"Took enough, did you?" he snapped.

Her eyes narrowed at his tone.

He couldn't prevent the growl that escaped from his throat.

Her eyes widened again before she moved to sweep her hair up into a sophisticated style, simply ignoring his question.

He didn't appreciate being ignored. "Don't you want more blood?" he pressed.

Lina stopped thrusting pins through her luscious hair and turned, staring at him with a mix of shock and wariness in her eyes. "I'm sure I don't know what you are talking about."

He smiled, lifting his hand and wiping his shoulder, but no blood remained. *How had it healed already?* The sudden lack of evidence made him stop for a moment. Should he question his own sanity? *No.* He wasn't wrong, he was certain of it. "You drank my blood when we came. How often do you require it?"

He could see the internal struggle going on within her, in the stiffness of her posture and the haunted look in her eyes.

"I didn't drink your blood, Benedict. Don't be absurd."

He laughed, but the sound held little humor as he pulled on his shirt. He staggered a little, still on a post orgasm high. A part of his brain knew he should be afraid of her, but he wasn't for some unknown reason. He was too furious with her for treating him like a fool to worry about his safety.

"Lina, you did. I saw my blood on your mouth, and now you look healthier, more vibrant. I even experienced some strange vision of an old man with long white hair while you were feeding on me."

She moved so quickly he didn't even see her. She went from being across the room, to standing right in front of him. Her blue eyes were wide as she moved around him slowly now, stalking him like a predator would do its prey. She looked shocked, wary, and curious.

"What did you just say?" she asked.

He swallowed, his bravado failing him for a moment. She was fast and if gossip was to be believed, she would be impossibly strong too. *She wouldn't hurt me, would she?* "Like I said, I saw an old man."

Lina shivered and leaned forward exposing her very real fangs.

Benedict jumped back, fear pulsing through him at the sight of the long white animal-like teeth. Then he stepped forward, inexplicably unable to keep his distance from her. She was still as beautiful as ever, and he was more than a little in awe of what she was. Did she want to feed on him again? *Perhaps...*

Some sort of perverse interest made him want to see it happen this time. So, he leaned into her and tilted his head away, exposing the source she so obviously craved. He couldn't stop the tremble in his muscles, but he held himself perfectly still. Pain coursed through him, again, and then the vision of her with the old man pierced his brain for the second time. The old man enfolded Lina in his arms now.

He gasped and jerked away, his head spinning with a strange and intoxicating pleasure.

Lina's mouth dripped with his blood, yet she didn't seem to be enjoying what she had taken from him. Her whole focus was centered on him. "What did you see?"

Benedict put his hand to the place where he expected to find proof of her feeding, but instead found a spot of blood against his skin, but no puncture wound. "How?" he breathed in wonder.

She shrugged, seemingly impatient with his line of questioning. "I secrete a healing fluid as I drink. Now answer me, Benedict."

Benedict shrugged also, imitating his beautiful lover, trying to fake a calm he didn't feel. *She really is a vampire.* Questions whirled in his mind. *How old is she? How often did she need to feed? How strong was she?*

"I saw you with the same man, again. Both of you were wearing purple robes."

Lina hissed a foreign word and flew across the room. She landed on a wooden pallet against the wall in a crouched position, defying the laws of nature, her hands trembling as she held them aloft from her body—just staring at them.

"I knew you were special," she uttered. "I *never* bring humans down here. But I couldn't help myself with you." She looked like a caged animal, worry, and fear surrounding her like a prison.

Any residual anger in Benedict's expression faded in the face of his lover's distress. He sighed; his feelings now secondary as his need to help her overruled them. He walked over to her side, squatted down in front of her, and cupped her exquisite face in his hands. "What's wrong, Lina? What does this mean?"

She swallowed audibly; her eyes uncertain. "I have heard stories of this. It happens when a vampire finds a human whose scent and blood is sweeter than any other they have ever tasted. If that human is their perfect match, they will not forget the bite as all others do. They will see the vampire's lived memories. In this case—my memories."

Benedict smiled awkwardly, wanting to soothe her worry. Inside, his stomach knotted in fear. Why was she talking like he was made for her? They had literally just met. *She can't possibly feel this way.* "So? Why the sad face, then?"

Lina flew away from him, faster this time.

His hands tingled with the loss of her skin against his palms. Benedict turned his body to see her land on the stairs.

"It is much more complex than you realize," she answered.

Benedict sighed and nodded. He didn't like being treated like a child. He could handle the truth. "Tell me. I'll listen."

Lina smiled like she'd found a treasure in the dark and Benedict's body responded to the beauty before him. She may not fulfill all of his needs, but his cock certainly loved her.

"How long until you next need to feed? A week?"

Lina shook her head, looking suddenly afraid again.

Benedict's own fear increased when he saw the look of hunger in her eyes. She wanted him again, too, but he sensed her reluctance. She could probably kill him if she drank too much too soon. He'd likely need time to recover from the loss.

"Two weeks?" he pressed.

She nodded slowly, though her expression didn't quite fit with her actions.

"I can go a month without blood and have done so many times before."

He inclined his head. She was being so considerate, a notion so at odds with the behavior of his Domme during sex. "But two weeks would be better?"

She smiled with impish appeal, her lush full lips turning up at the corners. She really was the most beautiful woman he had ever seen. Blue eyes, red lips, elegantly high cheek bones with flame red hair. She would put any duchess to shame.

"Yes, if you can handle this again." She motioned to her dungeon.

Benedict chuckled with real mirth and picked up his jacket, cravat, and boots. Unexpected joy floated through his veins at the mere idea of being with her again. "Lina, that was the best sex of my life," he said honestly. "We can do this every day if you promise not to kill me."

Her face turned solemn, and she stared at him for a long moment. "I must speak to an elder. I have never experienced this before."

Benedict's chest tightened unexpectedly, as though someone had clamped a vise on his ribs. Conflicting thoughts were flowing through him. He loved the idea of being special to her, being something that she wanted but had never experienced. Being used simply as a feeding and fucking toy was not what he wanted to be, though.

He reached her on the stairs and pulled her into him for a kiss.

Instantly, her tongue sought his out.

They clung to each other, lips, and tongues melding into one another until he was hard again.

She pressed herself into him, her nipples peaking against her dress.

"Another round?" he suggested, not entirely joking.

Lina smiled but pushed him up the stairs. "No, my pet, I need to think."

Benedict ascended the stairs much slower than he had descended. What awaited him up there except drunken friends and a world full of worries and responsibilities? Lina at least provided one glorious hour of escape. He turned to her when he heard her lock the door behind them. "Two weeks then."

Lina nodded and pulled him into her. Her lips were soft but so sure as they branded him, making a statement he'd not forget.

He broke away from her, panting, his cock rock solid again. It was not usually the way one walked out of a brothel, but that was exactly what he did.

CHAPTER

FOUR

Lina watched her intended blood mate walk away, then sagged against the door, her strength finally giving out. She licked her lips in remembrance and let a moan escape her. Never had she tasted blood so sweet or known such pleasure in a man's arms before. She knew the legends and always half feared the stories. Yet she hadn't believed them to be true. Not really. Now, she needed time to think, and she needed to speak to an elder. *What am I going to do?*

"Lina, please..."

She heard a woman's plaintive plea from a room above. A whisper meant only for her ears. She flew up the stairs and wrapped her hand around the drunken old man's throat that had caused her problems earlier.

The bastard had found Marie.

"I told you not to touch her," she snarled. "I warned you to leave her alone."

The man choked and spluttered, his shock and fear a horrible odor to her oversensitive senses.

Lina held him up in the air with one hand, squeezing gently. She could so easily kill him, and the world would be a better place without him, she was sure.

Marie—her dress ripped and her face swelling with a fresh, ugly bruise—put her hand gently on Lina's shoulder.

Her presence was calming, giving Lina enough reason to remove some of the pressure on the disgusting man's throat.

"Thank you, Lina, but I think this gentleman can leave, now. He won't ever return."

The man was almost white now, but he tried to nod to agree with what Marie was saying.

Repulsed, Lina dropped him. The thud of his body hitting the ground gave her some small satisfaction.

"Get out, and *never* come back. Or I will kill you."

The fat man crawled to the door, pulling his pants up back over his swollen belly as he moved. He was a sickening sight.

Lina growled.

He stood up, staggering as fast as his fat legs could carry him out of the room.

She took a deep steadying breath in an attempt to calm her tangled nerves. Her body had never felt more replete, so fully healthy. When Benedict had offered her his blood every day she had shuddered, physically restraining herself from flying across the room to him. The idea of just tying him up indefinitely appealed to her far too much.

The sex had been unbelievable. She rarely fucked humans as they could neither please her, nor survive the domination she loved to practice. Only male vampires permitted her that freedom, then fucked her *good* afterward. Unlike humans, they never tired—but she couldn't feed on them. So, the idea of having *all* that with a person she could feed on was enough to make her quiver right down to her now warm toes.

"Are you all right, Lina?"

She turned around to see Marie watching her, the beautiful whore who should have been a lady.

"Of course, Marie. How are you?"

The girl shrugged out of her ripped dress, standing in her chemise in the warm room. "I'm fine now. Thank you for rescuing me."

Lina stroked the girl's face gently and pulled her close for an embrace. "I will always come when you need me, Marie. Now, wash yourself and get some rest. We will repair your dress tomorrow."

Marie looked up at her, her young face worried in the candlelight.

"But the night isn't over, mistress. I can still earn some money."

Lina hushed her and directed her over to the washstand. "There will be more men tomorrow, Marie. But for now, lock your door, recover, and I will see you tomorrow evening. Be sure to ask Lizzie about your dress come the morning."

The beautiful girl nodded obediently and picked up the washcloth without another word, clearly quietly grateful for the night's reprieve.

Lina walked out the door with a wistful sigh and made her way downstairs. Her blood was on fire. She could still feel Benedict inside her and on her skin. It was truly amazing. There were going to be a lot of long, lonely days and nights between now and when she saw him again. *Oh, Benedict...*

CHAPTER

FIVE

Another night, another tedious ball. Benedict stood to the side of Lady Montan's ballroom and tried not to sigh out loud. How boring and extremely predictable his life had become. There were the beautiful young debutantes surrounded by the married matrons, like hens rounding up their little chicks. Every night it was the *same* music, the *same* food, the *same* people. He was sick of the monotony.

"Benedict." Lady Clover approached him and curtseyed.

He clenched his teeth together and stifled a groan. With practiced grace he forced himself to bow to her, despite the fact that this woman didn't deserve his manners. She was no lady by any stretch of the imagination. "Victoria," he said. "How lovely it is to see you."

She smiled and clasped his elbow, pressing herself closer than was socially appropriate.

With a note of discomfort, he could feel her large breasts bulging against his arm.

"I have a frightful headache, my lord," she complained. "Would you walk me along the balcony for some fresh air?" She looked up into his eyes, her devious request impossible to refuse and her tone hard to ignore.

Damn it. Begrudgingly, he had no choice but to agree. He was, after all, a gentleman. "Of course, my lady." He noticed the smirks of the other gentlemen as he walked by, and the disapproving looks from the older ladies. He usually didn't care what the women of the ton thought about him—but tonight he did. Everything about his life was annoying him this evening, and he found it strangely maddening.

"How is your husband, Victoria?" he asked, as it was polite to enquire.

She squeezed his arm and drew him further away from the ballroom doors. "He's away for the rest of the Season," she sighed. "I have missed you, Benedict." She dropped her hand and brazenly stroked his cock through his tailored pants.

It didn't even stir under her practiced touch. He stepped away from her, repulsed. "We finished our liaison months ago, Victoria. I have no wish to renew our agreement." In fact, he had never wanted her in the first place. He didn't like cuckolding another man—it wasn't honorable—but his pride had been pleased when she had approached him, and he hadn't been able to say 'no'.

Shock showed on her face, then anger sparked in her eyes. "I know you enjoyed our brief affair, Benedict. I can keep you well satisfied."

He smiled at Lady Victoria Clover in response. She may be dressed like a lady, but beneath the fine silk she was naught but a whore, no better than those who made an honest living with their flesh under Madam Lina's protection.

"I did Victoria and I thank you for thinking of me. However, I have no need for dalliances. I have employed a permanent mistress now."

Her pretty blue eyes flashed dangerously up at him, though she smiled sweetly. "You already had a mistress months ago, Benedict."

Benedict smiled back just as sweetly. That particular mistress was gone now, but should he tell Victoria the truth? He hadn't wanted to put the little witch in her place back then, he had thought he was better than that. Now, he didn't want to be. "Victoria, I have a *new* mistress who has no husband to slight and who satisfies my every need. I am now unavailable to you—and I will be keeping her *forever*." He blinked. Had he really just said such a telling statement out loud?

The true Victoria came out to play as she hissed at him. "You bastard."

He bowed at her and walked away, leaving the little hellcat to find someone else to dig her claws into. He was done.

Benedict stepped inside once again to find most of the married gentlemen sitting down to cards and cigars in the library. Finding an empty chair, he sank onto the hard leather. He was so very tired, his limbs felt like they were weighed down with lead.

"Benedict." An older man, who knew his father, addressed him and put a whiskey in front of him.

"Good evening, sir, thank you." Benedict grasped the glass and brought the cool crystal to his lips. The golden liquor slid down his throat with a soothing burn. Closing his eyes, he tried to ignore how much he ached for Lina. Anything that gave him pleasure, or pain, reminded him of her. He groaned and clenched his opposite hand in his lap.

"I saw Lady Clover get you onto the balcony. Didn't fall in with her plan I see?"

Benedict laughed, almost choking on his whiskey in surprise. Most men would not have said anything, but it seemed he had the good fortune of sitting next to the only man in the room who would. "I am not interested in filling her husband's position while he isn't looking. She can find someone else."

The old man puffed on his pipe and stared at Benedict with cold, assessing eyes. "Something has happened," he said matter-of-factly.

Benedict peered around the room at the drinking gentlemen. He listened as they discussed horse flesh, investments, and fashion. His stomach roiled. Was this what his future held? Night after night? He took another slug of whiskey. "It has, sir."

The man motioned for him to continue, his wizened eyes sharp and interested.

"I have met someone. A woman. She is different and will mercifully pull me away from this vapid world." He indicated to the gentlemen in the nearby proximity and swallowed the rest of his whiskey, gasping as the pain burned harder this time.

Puffing on his pipe, the older man looked at him and sat forward in his chair. "Your parents have gone through all their money, haven't they, son?"

Benedict flushed, but nodded. *No point trying to protect them now.*

"You don't like London society particularly well, Benedict. Do you?"

A smile trembled on Benedict's mouth as he remembered how much more fun it had been to play with the servants' children rather than the boys from school. His father had put a stop to that very quickly and beat him soundly for the misbehavior. He'd never quite fitted in anywhere.

"No, not particularly," he admitted with a wry laugh.

The older man leaned back in his chair and crossed his hands over his large chest. "Then what are you waiting for?" he asked. "If you have been given an opportunity to escape with a person you want above all else, then *go,* my boy! I had a similar opportunity many years ago and balked at the unknown. I missed my one and only chance at happiness." The gentleman's eyes were pained with regret. It seemed that kind of remorse was an unhealing wound.

Benedict stared at the man in front of him and tried to imagine him younger, full of life. Wanting to do more, be more. He couldn't picture such a thing, which was sad. Too much time had been lost. But it made him think. *Can I really do what I want?* Could he go back to Lina and see what she wanted to offer him? Could he balance both lives, or would he have to sacrifice one for the other?

He had so many questions, and few answers, but something inside him called out for change, for a different life. The other option. In only one night, Lina had lit a fire in his belly and in his soul that refused to be extinguished. He'd barely had a taste of her, and he wanted so much more.

Benedict didn't know if Lina wanted to keep him or just use him to feed on, but he wanted to take the risk and find out. The hardest thing was in admitting the truth to himself. *I don't really care what she intends.* Mere moments in her arms were better than years of pomp and society in the real world.

CHAPTER

SIX

Antony was enjoying his usual prowl around London when he smelled something so spectacular as to be close to divinity. No one had ever smelled so good to him—not even Malcolm. His heart sank at the memory of his past lover. Clenching his jaw, he pushed the pain far, far down.

He would have this juicy prey and taste the blood that throbbed in those delicious veins, no matter the cost.

Picking up his pace, Antony walked faster while trying not to draw attention to himself. The man who smelled so very delicious was almost at Lina's brothel now. *How predictably boring*. It seemed his prey was going to be easily caught this evening.

SEVEN

B enedict stepped back into Lina's brothel—alone this time. Fourteen days almost to the minute since he had walked into the whorehouse for the first time. The muscles in his legs trembling with excitement, he mounted the door stoop and pushed open the heavy door.

Lina's dungeon provided an escape for him from the crazy world which was his life. When he was with her, he forgot his money stresses and his parents' expectations. He had endured the worst yet, this past week. His family was in insurmountable debt, and everyone in the ton knew it. Yet his parents continued to expect the same standard of living they had always enjoyed. They were in so much financial trouble that it was depressing and overwhelming to dwell on.

Benedict knew beyond any doubt that his parents wanted him to marry an heiress, a woman with enough wealth to pull his family out of their dire situation, but he just couldn't sacrifice what was left of his freedom. *Not yet.*

He stepped inside the warm, well-lit main room and scanned it for his vampire. The last time they were together he had provided her with the blood she needed, and she had given him moments of pure bliss. He couldn't wait to make the same exchange again.

Disappointment hit him punch to the gut when he realized she wasn't there. Benedict walked over to her male guard and house butler. "Excuse me, but where's Lina?"

The man looked him up and down with an arrogance unbecoming of a servant. "Unavailable, sir. Would you like one of the other girls?"

Benedict clenched his teeth, his jaw aching as he waited for the anger to recede. He had gone weeks without her, without any other woman and she was going to deny him *now*? He couldn't possibly bear it! "She asked me to return in two weeks," he said, trailing his fingers down his neck, hoping the butler would understand the underhanded gesture and make the connection.

The man's eyes bulged as he watched Benedict's hand linger near where bite marks should be.

Yes. He understood.

"My apologies," he said quickly. "I will find out if that includes you, sir."

Benedict nodded.

The butler bowed and hurried from the room.

Turning, he stood as the ill-mannered had, watching the men with Lina's women. She protected them, he knew she did. And he really liked that about her. No one of his social standing would think twice about the serving class, and even less about the women forced into this sort of situation to make ends meet. But Lina cared. That made her exceptional.

"Benedict." Lina's voice curled into his ear.

He turned, expecting to find a welcoming smile on her face.

Instead, she looked like a sour faced madam, her full lips tilted down.

He frowned as the excited butterflies in his belly were crushed by the weight of his disappointment. He had counted every minute of the last two weeks and had thought she would feel the same way.

"What's wrong, Lina?" he ventured.

Lina grabbed his hand, her skin cool against his, and pulled him toward the entrance to her dungeon.

His heart rate sped up. She didn't look like she wanted him here but perhaps she still did?

"You must go, Benedict. Come back tomorrow."

Hurt filled his chest. She couldn't be serious, could she? "Sorry?"

A whoosh of air surrounded him as a male materialized in front of him.

"Who's the human, Lina?" he asked, intrigued.

His Domme looked pained as she gestured to the beautiful man beside her. "Benedict, this is Antony. Antony, this is Benedict."

There was no mistaking what this attractive male companion of Lina's was. Everything about him reeked of seduction and predatory power. *Antony is a vampire.* There wasn't a single doubt in Benedict's mind.

Antony inhaled and groaned with lust.

The sound echoed in Benedict's ears and went straight to his balls.

The vampire's eyes widened, and his nostrils flared.

Benedict could smell this new vampire's arousal and knew it was for him. It was a very strange sensation to smell lust and it was even stranger when Benedict's body hardened in response to it. He'd never wanted a man before in his whole life. Why would Antony appeal to him?

"A new pet, Lina?" asked the vampire, his voice almost a purr.

She dropped her eyes and lowered her voice. "My intended blood mate," she said by way of explanation.

The words meant nothing to Benedict, but he liked the sound of them. *Blood mate?* He rolled the words around in his mind. It sounded important somehow. A thing of meaning, a position of status, perhaps?

Antony looked back at him with renewed interest.

Benedict felt the tension in Lina, watched her tremble slightly under Antony's regard. *Is she afraid of the new vampire?* He wondered. *Or is she worried for me?* He couldn't tell. He must protect himself and Lina, also. He would do the gentlemanly thing and leave, just as she had requested. He would return another time, however. "I can come back tomorrow, Lina. I'm sorry, I must have misunderstood." Benedict bowed and began backing away.

Not even a breath later and strong male arms wrapped around his chest, pinning Benedict's arms firmly to his sides. Antony's supernatural strength surrounded him. "Not so fast, there, beautiful boy. You smell *delicious*."

Then he was free, and Lina was holding Antony up against the wall, her strength obviously superior to the well-built male vampire. Her face was hard, her eyes narrowed and flaring in anger. She was an awesome sight to behold.

"He is *mine*," she hissed. "You know the rules, Antony."

Antony groaned and pouted. He really was a beautiful thing.

Benedict's cock began to swell of its own accord as he imagined touching the other man. *What a lovely mouth he has.*

"Can't I have a taste too, Lina? Please? We could share," Antony begged.

Benedict flushed, his body heating in unusual ways at the idea of being shared between two beautiful vampires. He had never been attracted to another man before, but this one smelled divine. His arousal was evident, and Benedict wanted to reach out and touch him.

Lina turned her head toward Benedict and narrowed her eyes, inhaling deeply. Her eyebrows rose high as a small smile graced her lovely face, "You want him to join us?"

Benedict blushed deeply, the heat on his throat and cheeks embarrassing. He couldn't hide his arousal from her, but he was worried about the unknown. Afraid of the strength this male possessed. What would he be made to do in a sexual situation with the two of them? "Will he hurt me?" he asked in return, echoing what he had asked *her* just two weeks past.

Lina smiled with an evil glint to her blue eyes and looked back at Antony. "Two rules. You obey me at all times. And you only take a small amount of blood. If you dare hurt him, I *will* kill you, make no mistake."

Benedict blinked with surprise at his lover. *She is serious*, he realized. Perhaps she did care for him as he was beginning to care for her?

Antony nodded enthusiastically despite the clear threat. His white, pointed fangs elongated and slid across his bottom lip in readiness.

Benedict stepped back to let Lina pass. His heart thumped hard against his rib cage and adrenaline surged in his veins, making him feel strong and ready to run if need be. *What have I just agreed to?*

Lina opened her door and gestured for them to enter.

Benedict stepped through the opening first, his breath hitching as he descended all fifty-seven steps. He counted this time. Once he reached the bottom he began to undress, unwilling to look at what the other two were doing for fear would get the better of him. Despite knowing they would smell it on him, it wasn't controllable.

When he was completely naked, he turned to face them only to find them still watching him. His body was shaking despite the heat of the room, but he refused to run. Not that he'd get anywhere. Instead, he bit his lip, took a deep breath, and simply stood in front of them, his cock erect and ready for their attention.

Lina pointed to a wooden cross that stood in one corner of the room. "Up on the cross, my pet. Antony, help him," she instructed.

EIGHT

Before he could move, the male vampire picked Benedict up around the waist as easily as if he were a paper doll, his hands cool and smooth.

Benedict had to stifle the groan that rose from his throat when the vampire deliberately rubbed against his aching erection as he placed him on the cross with his back against the wood.

The beautiful vampire smiled as he tied Benedict's wrists and feet in fast, sure motions that could be matched by no mere human.

Benedict's heart galloped in his chest. He was tied once again and was completely helpless. With Antony so close, he could appreciate the sexiness of his lips and the smoothness of his skin. He ached for Antony to touch him again, to have the handsome vampire kiss him. But his tangible fear of the unknown stopped him from expressing his desire out loud.

Lina appeared in front of him, smiling with lust clear in her blue eyes. "You want his mouth, my pet?"

How had she known exactly what he had been thinking? He swallowed hard, still unable to admit to such a thing aloud. "Lina, you're in charge down here." No sooner were the words out of his mouth, he regretted them. Benedict knew how two men fucked—and he couldn't do that. *She wouldn't make me, would she?*

"Strip, Antony."

The male vampire was naked by the time Benedict finished blinking. His sculpted body was incredible to see. It was the color of pale milk and literally ripped with muscle. His cock was much bigger than Benedict's, too, and curved upward.

Benedict gasped. He couldn't handle something that big. *What do I even do with it?*

Lina chuckled and spoke directly into his ear. "Do not fear, my lover. He will not hurt you. I promise."

Benedict exhaled, relief swamping him like a breath of fresh air. He should have known Lina would protect him. There was no need to fear. She was a caring Domme.

Lina picked up her crop and pointed at the male vampire with it. "Suck on him until he comes, Antony."

Benedict gasped loudly, pulling at his restraints. He couldn't have that. His secret desires were not meant to be fulfilled! "No, Lina. Please don't make him. I don't want that."

She smiled, the wicked side of her Domme nature returning. "You wanted his mouth, my pet, now feel him."

Antony sank to his knees.

Benedict turned his head away, closing his eyes so he couldn't witness what was about to happen.

Wet warmth engulfed his cock head and he moaned as a wave of pleasure washed over him. Amazing suction and a relentless tongue pushed him close to the edge within seconds. Benedict hesitantly opened his eyes and looked down.

The beautiful man with dark eyes and darker hair worked his cock with the skill of someone who had done so countless times before. He sucked, licked and pulled on the shaft with strong movements.

Pleasure pulsed through his body in all-consuming waves. Over and over the sensations made him cry out, and he'd pull on his restraints. The feelings tightened his balls and made his skin tingle. He wasn't going to be able to control it for much longer. He loved watching Antony suck him, more than he imagined he possibly could. It more than doubled his pleasure.

He arched his back and looked over at his Domme, pleading with her for help. "I'm going to come, Lina. Make him stop."

She smiled kindly but shook her head in the negative, denying him his request. "No stopping, my pet. Now, come for me."

Having been given permission, Benedict groaned as his sac tightened and his body shuddered with his impending orgasm. He closed his eyes and let Antony's mouth push him up to and over the edge.

Lina was behind him, at his neck, kissing him as his seed pulsed out of him. As Benedict opened his mouth and screamed in ecstasy, Antony swallowed him down, and Lina bit into the side of his neck, drinking his blood as surely as his hot seed rushed into the other man's luscious mouth.

Benedict shuddered and all of his senses seemed to disappear as he floated on a cloud of pure bliss. How long he remained there, beyond himself, he wasn't sure. But he slowly became more aware of himself. When he opened his eyes, he found both vampires cradling his sweaty, sated body.

Lina was still at his neck, kissing his skin and stroking his hair. The effect was soothing and erotic all at once.

Antony was still on his knees, licking Benedict's fast deflating cock.

"You taste fucking divine," said Antony as he licked Benedict once more.

Benedict shuddered with another echo of his orgasm, then he looked up at his gorgeous vampire playmate. "What next, Lina?"

Lina kissed Benedict's neck once more, her lips soft against his healed skin. "Make us a comfortable bed, Antony."

The handsome vampire flew around the room in a flurry.

While Lina slowly undid Benedict's wrists and ankles.

The blood flowed back into his limbs as his arms dropped like lead weights, the ache in them intensifying.

"Are you okay, my pet?" she asked.

Benedict shook his head, disappointment flooding him. He was ashamed of his behavior; how selfish he had been! Taking his own pleasure in such a short amount of time. *How will I be of any use to my lover now?* "I didn't want to come like that."

She laughed musically and led him over to the floor, now covered in pillows and soft silks. "You will come however I wish for you to, my pet. Now, eat me." She dropped the dress from her body and fell gracefully into the pillows, legs spread wide, inviting him.

Benedict gazed down at her, his heart filling with happiness. Her body was truly incredible to look upon and he was honored to be the one to do so. She was tight and firm, yet still soft and feminine. He couldn't resist her.

Benedict dropped to his knees, then moved to his belly so his face was level with her pussy. He stared at her, admiring the pink flesh, the soft lips, and luscious opening. Inhaling her musky scent, he groaned as his soft cock began filling with blood again. He couldn't believe it. He had never recovered so quickly before.

He didn't dwell on why, just leaned forward to taste her pussy lips coated with her thick, creamy essence. He hummed in his throat and drank greedily. Her flavor was like nothing he had ever had before, and he was hungry for more.

"Antony, I want to taste your cock," Lina said between gasps and moans.

Benedict looked up from his meal to see the male vampire lie down next to them, Antony's head close to Benedict's, his cock near Lina's face. The butterflies in his belly returned. The other vampire added so much to their dynamic, in both looks and intensity. Benedict had never felt anything remotely similar.

Lina leaned forward and sucked Antony's cock into her mouth.

Arousal, hot and strong swept through Benedict, watching his Domme sucking another male's cock at the same time as he licked her clit. It made it even better that it was Antony's huge, perfect cock and the man in question was close enough to touch.

Benedict bent his head again to his task, flicking his tongue over the sensitive bud of her clit; then drawing his hand up, he thrust two long fingers deep into her pussy.

Her body wrapped around him in response. She was hot, tight, and *so* wet. Lina groaned; the sound deliciously muffled by her actions.

Antony's cool hands settled on Benedict's back.

He shuddered and continued to pleasure Lina's pussy. This was hands-down the most erotic experience of his life. The moans of the two vampires rang in his ears.

Antony stroked his skin, lazily drawing imaginary patterns with his teasing fingers.

Lina arched her back and cried out, the sound like a siren song. "I need you both, now. *Stop*, Benedict."

Benedict obeyed without question. He quit lapping at her swollen flesh and raised himself up on all fours, his balls aching for release. He was amazed at how hard his cock was again.

"Where do you want me, Lina?" Antony asked, his face strained with desire.

"On your back, you get my pussy."

In the next instant Antony was on his back.

Lina impaled herself on the vampire's massive, curved cock. She groaned and pushed down, shuddering in pleasure.

"Fuck..." Benedict said on a breath, unable to tear his gaze away.

Pre-cum began seeping out of Benedict's cock. The picture the two vampires made together looked incredible.

"My pet, get behind me," panted Lina.

Benedict moved as instructed but was confused about what she wanted.

Lina leaned forward and pulled her ass cheeks open with both hands.

The sight of her filled with the other vampire was impossibly tempting. Perhaps he could lick them where they were joined?

"Inside my ass, quickly, Benedict! I can't hold out much longer."

He hesitated. *She isn't being serious?* "Really? I won't hurt you?"

Lina groaned and shook her head emphatically. "No, female

vampires are designed to take two cocks. I'm already ready and wet there, *please.*"

Something completely primal took hold of Benedict when she offered him that part of herself. He placed a hand on her lower back and pushed her down, closer to Antony, then lined his cock up with her ass. He pressed in an inch and groaned as her tight wet hole allowed him access. *I'll never last here!*

Moaning, Lina pushed back against him, opening for him and relaxing.

Benedict slid in slowly, his fear of hurting her warring with his need to claim her completely. Pushing in up to the base, he moved slowly, allowing her time to stretch and grow accustomed to his presence.

She gasped and started to shake. "For the love of God! Move, both of you, now!"

Benedict felt Antony move as the thin layer between their cocks seemed to disappear. He could feel everything. His balls tightened as his cock head throbbed with unparalleled pleasure.

Benedict moved out when Antony thrust up, and then back in when Antony moved down. Between them they established a good rhythm and were soon fucking her and giving her a steady pounding.

The sounds of their grunts, gasps, and slapping skin echoed around the room.

"I'm coming, my pet, please," Lina gasped.

Benedict knew exactly what she needed and fell forward onto her. He held himself up by his arms as he thrust deeply into her ass one last time.

She turned her head, arching her back, and bit into his neck as she came with terrifying strength. Her body gripped them both, spasming over and over, undulating like a wave and forcing them over their own cliffs into the oblivion of ecstasy.

Antony screamed first.

The vibration echoed over the skin of Benedict's wrist.

Antony sunk his fangs into Benedict, taking what he promised.,

The pure taboo and sinful pleasure of being fed on by two beautiful vampires pushed Benedict into an even greater level of orgasm. Something he didn't think was even physically possible. But his body exploded in a pleasure that stole the legs from under him and he fell properly onto his mate; his seed pulsing out of him and into her in hot, long bursts of breath-taking delirium.

Antony smiled up at a grinning Lina. That had been the most incredible experience for him. The sex alone had been mind-boggling, but to taste Benedict's blood at the critical point as well.. That had made the experience exceptional. He still felt the heat buzzing through his veins. And in truth, he couldn't remember feeling this healthy in decades.

She spoke first. "I think he's lost consciousness."

He chuckled, the noise rusty and strange to his ears. He hadn't made a sound like that in a century. "Well, if I was still human, I may have too. He got one more orgasm than me." Antony smiled again as he ran his tongue over his lips. He could still taste Benedict's seed. It was almost as spectacular as his blood. *I wonder if Lina would allow me some more of both?*

Lina shifted on him, looking uncomfortable.

He knew she could accommodate them both easily, but she was sandwiched between the two of them with—Benedict's limp body on top of her. Personally, he loved the feel of their combined weight pressing into him. "Is he really your blood mate, Lina?" His brows furrowed together, but he couldn't prevent it as his quiet concern grew. He was worried for his longtime friend and lover.

Lina smiled at him, pure happiness shining in her eyes.

A sense of relief washed over Antony. They had been lovers, friends, and a great support for each other for as long as Lina had been a vampire. He would miss her terribly if she chose to focus solely on Benedict. *I don't know if I could stand that...*

"You'll see when he wakes up," she said simply.

As though her words had caused the very thing to happen, Benedict began to stir.

A strange feeling of confusion swept over Antony, and he frowned again. Why was he feeling Benedict's emotions?

Benedict gasped and planted his hands on Lina's hips, pushing up. He eased out of her and fell into a kneeling position beside them. "Lina, did I hurt you?"

Antony shook his head.

Lina just laughed and caressed Benedict's face. *Hurt her?* Benedict obviously knew nothing about their kind at all. She was a four-hundred-year-old vampire and had one of the most powerful creators they knew. She eased off Antony's now softened cock and moved over to straddle Benedict.

Antony rolled over and got to his feet, stretching his ancient muscles in sublime enjoyment. That had been truly incredible, he actually felt sated. When was the last time that had happened?

When he turned around again, he wondered if he should perhaps stay a little longer.

Benedict sat further back on his heels and had wrapped his arms around Lina's waist as she straddled him.

They were aroused again.

Antony could smell them both and it heated his own blood.

Lina stroked her new pet's face while she spoke. "You cannot hurt me, Benedict. Tell me what you saw."

Antony couldn't wait to hear this. He had never truly believed in blood mates, before. Not the sort the Originals talked about, at least.

Benedict flushed and looked back at him.

Antony felt that look down to his belly, kicking him into awareness. Something very dangerous was about to be said.

Benedict turned his attention to Lina. "I saw you having sex with the old man in the robes."

Antony blinked, shocked. *Perhaps some of the stories were true?*

"Then when Antony bit me, I saw him having sex with another human male. He had orange-red hair and blue eyes."

Antony hissed and fell back a step. "You lie!" Shock and anger hit him hard and unexpectedly. He jumped closer to the pallet of pillows and stared at the entwined couple. There was no way Benedict could be telling the truth. There's no way he could have known! *Lina must have said something.* He forced himself to calm down just a little before he cleared his throat and asked for clarification. "What did you say?"

Hands fisted on each side, Antony struggled to rein his temper in. *How dare Lina share that sort of private information?* He had lost his intended mate more than a hundred years ago and he had barely spoken of him since.

Benedict looked up at Lina with pleading eyes.

Antony knew that look wasn't faked. Benedict was afraid. *What the hell is going on?*

Lina turned to look at him calmly. "I just wanted to show you our connection, Antony. Please do not be upset. If you fed on him again, he would not sense your memories. It must have been because we were both in his blood at the same time."

Antony took a big step forward, wanting to test her theory.

Lina moved to her feet in front of Benedict, acting as a shield and blocking Antony access. "He has been fed on enough tonight. You know that," she said, her voice firm.

Antony's fear was beginning to rise, but so was his hope. It was rare to have a triple blood bond and even rarer to have more than one intended mate. But if he had another? he needed to know! "I just want to find out..."

Lina grabbed him by the shoulders and shook him. She was

younger than he was, but her maker had been one of the Originals. That alone made her one of the strongest vampires on the planet. He knew he was no true match for her when it came down to it.

"He will not be able to see him, Antony. I know you regret your decision, but Benedict cannot bring him back. I am sorry."

The words hurt to hear, even worse because Lina did not understand. He knew Malcolm could never be brought back, that wasn't what hurt so much. He knew that he had lost the one person who was his only intended mate.

But there was something about Benedict, the sweetness of his blood, his scent. All of it fitted together like a neat little puzzle box and Antony needed to find out if there was something more to it. He needed to talk to an elder, to find out if he was going crazy with jealousy and longing, or if it was truly possible—that he, Lina, and Benedict could be blood mates.

"I will be back, Lina." He ripped out of her hold, picked up his clothes, and flew out of the building.

CHAPTER

TEN

Lina turned back to the man she knew to be her destined mate and waited for the main door to the dungeon to close. It didn't. *Childish prick*. She would not be as foolish as Antony was. She would not let Benedict go.

Benedict stood, his beautiful body rippling as he seemed to want to move. He seemed unsure of her. Wary somehow.

She moved over to him and stroked her nails across one of his tight little nipples. "Let's lay down again, pet."

Benedict nodded and sank back to the pillows.

Lina retrieved a blanket and covered them both, lying on her side to face him.

Benedict's eyebrows furrowed in thought. "Did I say something wrong to Antony?" he asked. He reached over, stroking her face gently.

Lina leaned into the caress, love winging through her chest. She had not been shown tenderness like this since before she had been turned. Lust, yes, paternal caring, yes. But true tenderness from a lover was a very rare commodity, indeed. Especially due to her need to Domme them.

"No, Benedict. Antony is just sensitive when it comes to Malcolm."

Benedict ran his fingertips down the bridge of her nose, exploring every inch.

Lina wanted to purr in enjoyment.

"The man I saw?"

Lina sighed and nodded. She didn't really want to talk about this now, didn't want Benedict to know just how strongly she felt about him. However, she must. "Yes, you described Malcolm perfectly."

Benedict leaned forward and kissed her gently on the lips.

Lina's belly trembled; she wanted him again.

"Malcolm was Antony's mate, his intended mate for all time. But Antony refused to believe that the legends were true, despite all the signs. He was scared and he fought their connection. Especially as his mate was male..."

Benedict shuffled closer and smiled kindly at her. He liked to listen, how unusual for a man. "What happened?"

Lina looked away from Benedict's intense stare, fearful herself now. This conversation was going to lead into waters she herself did not want to venture. "Antony moved away, went searching for something else—someone else—hoping to forget what he'd felt. He couldn't though, no matter how hard he tried."

Benedict leaned forward and kissed her gently on the neck.

Lina shuddered as warmth curled through her body. She must finish the story. It would stand as a warning for all vampires who knew of the blood mate story. "When he returned to claim his lover, Malcolm had died."

Benedict inhaled sharply, going pale. "They both lost."

Lina nodded sadly. "It's worse for Antony, of course. Malcolm would have missed Antony as any man in love would, but Antony had tasted his mate's blood, claimed him in the flesh... For a vampire there is nothing more binding. He will mourn Malcolm for as long as he lives, which could be for several centuries more."

Benedict nodded, his quick intellect putting everything together.

Lina watched it happen, relieved, and yet terrified. She couldn't *make* Benedict bond with her.

"How old are you?" he asked.

Lina laughed, relieved for a moment. Her cheeky human was back.

"I have lost track a little over the years, but four hundred years or so."

Benedict inhaled sharply; his eyes wary. "And have you found your mate in that time?"

She smiled, leaned forward, and kissed *him* for the first time. His lips were soft and yielding. Ready to receive and give pleasure in return.

Lina pushed Benedict onto his back and straddled him, feeling him grow hard beneath her. This was the most important moment of her existence, and her hands shook as she cupped her lover's face in her palms. "I found him just two weeks ago. I have been very lonely for you, Benedict." She sat up on him and moved her long hair off her shoulders to give him the best view of her body.

Benedict smiled up at her sweetly, a slightly incredulous look in his eyes. "You want me?" His hands came up to cup her breasts, stroking the plump flesh before squeezing each nipple in turn.

She moaned at the pleasure, intense and instant. Lina's fangs began to elongate, and she closed her eyes for a moment, forcing them back. "Yes, we will be mated, and I will turn you so that we can be together forever." She began moving her wet pussy against Benedict's cock, hoping it would harden faster. She needed him again, though she needed to abstain from feeding from him.

She was still lightheaded from his blood, the strength of it intoxicating and dizzying. She had never tasted anything better. It was richer than any wine, and more decadent than any flavor of food she had ever tasted as a human. He would be her life source until she turned him. *Then we will feed on other humans together.*

Benedict's hands stilled her movements.

Lina opened her eyes.

Benedict was glaring up at her. "What do you mean, when you turn me?"

Lina focused her energy and realized Benedict wasn't feeling as she was, complete and happy. He was angry. She didn't understand that at all. She was offering him immortality! *What man wouldn't yearn for such a thing?* "How can we be together forever if I don't turn you?" Lina cupped her lover's jaw, willing him to understand.

He frowned, his flesh going soft beneath her.

Worry began to unfurl in Lina like the petals of a dying daisy falling away into darkness.

"But what about my life?" he asked. "My parents? I have so many loose ends to tie up, Lina. Why can't you marry me and just live with me for a few years?"

Panic deep within Lina's belly had her digging her nails into Benedict's face unknowingly.

He jerked away with a groan of pain. Blood dripped down the side of his face in gentle red rivulets.

"My pet, I'm so sorry." She extended her tongue and licked up the drops from her lover's skin and groaned in bliss as her fangs extended again. She could die tomorrow and know that she had tasted the sweetest blood on the planet. When Lina finally opened her eyes again, she found Benedict staring at her with a puzzled look on his face.

"What does that taste like?" he asked.

She smiled. How could she explain to a human what Heaven tasted like? "Like the richest food, or the nicest wine. It's the best thing I have ever tasted."

Benedict quirked an eyebrow, lifted her up and rolled out from under her.

Why is he acting like this?

"So, I am just... your food?" He growled as he got to his feet.

Lina chuckled and stood also.

He looked angry and he had no reason to be.

She was offering him immortality and he reduced himself to merely sustenance? "Oh yes, my lover, you are my food. Your blood keeps me alive in this moment. But you are also my reason for existing, and I offer you everything I am because of that." She circled him, proudly displaying her naked body. Lina knew she was lithe, supple and voluptuous, a lethal combination for most men. If she ever wanted to seduce a man, that time was *now*.

Benedict's eyes followed her, dropping to her nipples when she thrust them up. "I need time to think about this." He began pulling on his clothes.

Lina acted on instinct, fear threading through her chest. She climbed up onto him, wrapping her arms around his neck and her legs around his waist. "Don't leave, Benedict." Lina began kissing her mate, his muscled neck, his soft lips, his turned cheek. Anywhere she could reach. She had to make him understand how she felt.

"I can't lose you like Antony lost Malcolm, please... sweetheart..."

Benedict groaned with obvious frustration and turned, pushing her up against the wall. The stone was hard and solid at her back.

Lina clung to that for strength.

"I have to go home." Benedict grunted at her as he ground his body against her still naked form.

Lina could smell his arousal, his now hard cock pressing against her.

"Yes, my pet," she whispered into his ear encouragingly, even as she maneuvered herself to take him again. "Now, fuck me."

Benedict moaned, gripped her ass with both hands and plunged into her pussy.

She screamed aloud, arching her back to pull him deeper as he withdrew and thrust into her again. Lina cried out against the feelings flowing through her. Every time they fucked, her feelings for him grew. The need to protect him and bind him to her was almost over-whelming.

Benedict moved faster and harder, his cock pushing her toward another orgasm as he gripped her hips and held her hostage against the wall.

She closed her eyes, allowing his feelings to wash over her.

His arousal, his need, his passion for her, all buffeted her already overloaded system. He was everything she had ever needed and he couldn't leave her, *he couldn't.*

"Fuck, Lina, I'm going to come..."

Lina tilted her pelvis to take him even deeper and reached between them to flick her clit with her own fingers, once, twice, tightening the already highly strung coil inside her body.

She felt him swell, and felt her own body pause in its pleasure, waiting for him.

Benedict groaned and thrust deep, his orgasm triggering hers.

Lina moaned when she felt the warm spill of his seed. She shook against the wall in the arms of her lover. Her fangs elongated, but she turned her head away, unwilling to seek out the blood that called to her. She had taken too much today already.

Benedict leaned forward, shaking in his aftermath, too. He kissed her neck gently,

The gesture was enough to make Lina want to cry.

"Incredible."

Lina could barely keep her eyes open. She was satisfied to her very core, and it was far too close to sunrise. *I need to rest.* "My pet, would you stay with me?"

Benedict pulled out of her and gently put her on her feet.

Lina staggered to the mound of pillows and blankets, collapsing on top of them.

Benedict soon lay down next to her, her warm sweaty skin the perfect place to be. "Do you sleep all day?" he asked, stroking her cheek.

Lina was half way asleep already. She curled into his heated body and sighed happily. She had never spent her day resting with a human. In truth it had been a long time since she spent the daytime with anyone at all. "Yes, I do. My butler will lock the door at the top for my safety, then someone will reopen it again at sundown."

Lina felt Benedict's panic, but his resistance to leave her was pleasing.

"I can't stay all day…" he protested.

She smiled to herself and pulled the blanket up over them. "You are safe, my pet. You're home in my arms. Now, you have come three times and provided us with sustenance. Sleep. You deserve rest."

Lina felt Benedict relax beneath her and she let a deep healing rest take over her body.

Benedict awoke, sated, warm and completely relaxed. He blinked twice, trying to remember what had taken place last night. Feeling Lina's warm, sumptuous body still clinging to him jolted his mind to recall the memories. He was her blood mate and she wanted to turn him into a vampire. *Oh God!*

Looking down, he couldn't stop the smile from forming on his face. Nor could he ignore the feeling of complete peace that enveloped him like a blanket. He'd never felt like this, never knew such a feeling existed. Every other morning of his life he awoke with a feeling of dread, his worry and stress crowding his thoughts before his eyes had even opened to drink in the morning sunlight.

Amazing what some incredible sex and being wanted by a powerful vampire could do! He hadn't realized he wanted to feel so needed. He ran a hand up and down Lina's smooth, warm back. *What am I going to do?*

He wasn't letting her go, and she wouldn't let him go, he was sure of that. The strength of her conviction and her belief that she would not ever recover from losing him was very overwhelming on one level. But on another however, he felt relieved. He had struggled these past two weeks, being away from her, and he knew his feelings were growing with each and every hour they spent together.

Antony added another level to their encounter too. If Benedict was honest, he had probably enjoyed having Antony with them *more* than he had enjoyed sex with just Lina alone. Absurd really, but true. He would have to figure out how he felt so he knew what to do when the choice was there to be made.

Lina's warm tongue licked his nipple.

Heat infused his groin. How could he want her again? His appetite for her surpassed every other encounter in his sexual history.

She sucked his nipple completely into her mouth and used her sharp teeth on the flesh.

Gasping, he ran his fingers through her hair, the thick red tresses silky soft.

She moved further down, kissing his belly and using her tongue to taste the indent of his navel.

Benedict closed his eyes and held his breath as her lips caressed his cock, straining to meet her. They needed to get out of this dungeon. He needed to get his thoughts together and he couldn't think while they were being as intimate as this.

Her hot mouth enveloped the head, her tongue running around the tip, before tasting his slit which was weeping pre-cum for her already.

He groaned, squeezing her skull; knowing he couldn't really hurt her made everything so much easier and that much hotter. "Lina!" He moaned.

She took almost his entire length into her mouth, then came back off him again. With a smile, she looked up, catching his eye. "Stay still, pet."

He groaned again as she sucked harder, pain tingeing his pleasure.

She moved, and suddenly he was pinned to the floor, his arms stretched above his head by a rope.

How did she do that?

Lina grinned down at him as she lowered herself onto his cock, one agonizing inch at a time. Tight, wet heat squeezed him.

Benedict groaned as he tugged on his bonds. The added level of restraint and feeling of powerlessness only heightened his arousal. And until Lina, never in a million years would he have guessed that he was into bondage. It'd just never been on the cards before—but love with his vampire mate was different.

Lina fully engulfed him, her hot pussy clenching around him.

He closed his eyes, squeezing them tight against the onslaught of sensation.

"Open your eyes, my pet," she commanded.

He didn't comply, he couldn't. Lina overwhelmed his senses on too many levels. He was a little afraid. Without warning both of his nipples were pinched and twisted sharply. Pain sliced through him at the same time as she began to move. His eyes flew open, the pleasure soon over-riding the pain, mixing and making it stronger.

"You are mine, Benedict, do you understand?" She moved slowly, staring deep into his eyes.

He shook his head.

She squeezed her inner muscles.

"You are my pet. Preordained. Destined. You are meant to be mine." Lina gripped his cock and moved on him, up, down, faster and more aggressively. Her breasts moved with her every bounce, their abundant flesh tempting him, as if begging for his touch.

But he couldn't move. "Lina."

She groaned and moved faster still, rotating her hips on the downward grind to give him an extra level of pleasure. "Yes, my pet?"

He groaned, his ball sac tightening beneath her. "I need to touch you."

She laughed; the sound musical.

He moaned as she rippled around him. He was going crazy—positively wild with lust. Every inch of his body was screaming with raw, primal pleasure.

"You don't need to do anything except fill me with your cum." She threw back her head and moved even faster, using her supernatural speed, moaning in time with her own building pleasure.

Benedict struggled in vain against his bonds some more, sweat breaking out on his face, chest, and arms as physical exertion mingled with ecstasy.

She was unrelenting, her movements designed to push him over the edge fast. Linda was showing him who was in charge, and he could do nothing to stop her.

His traitorous body loved every second of her domination and his heart cried out for more. "Fuck…" He planted his feet on the floor and began thrusting up, pushing her body higher and higher, pounding into her.

She gripped him and cried out.

He let go, divine, sinful pleasure shooting up his cock and inside her. Groaning, he shuddered and pulled on his restraints.

Meanwhile, Lina moaned, rocking back and forth, milking every last drop out of him.

When the tidal wave of sensation died down to a more manageable level, he lay there panting, just trying to catch his breath. *How can I want her like this, all of the time?* His heart kicked out at him; something was missing…

Lina collapsed on top of him, her head tucked into the crook of his neck.

Her hot breath against his skin caused a shiver to course down his spine. He shook his head to clear his poor muddled head.

He had to make this right somehow. He couldn't be falling in love with Lina, want her above all others, and *not* marry her. It wasn't right. "Come home with me."

She lifted her head, her eyes narrowed. "We could just stay here, Benedict," she purred.

He groaned and tugged on the ropes. He really didn't want to be tied up for this conversation.

She looked up and moved, her speed too fast for him to follow with his eyes. He was untied and she was laid back on top of him before a moment had even passed.

He stretched his arms down, allowing the blood to flow again.

They ached in the strangest way. He sat up slowly, taking her with him. Should he try to bring her into his world? "Marry me."

Even as he said the words Benedict knew such a thing would never work. How could he marry the madam of a brothel? A mistress of the night? The scandal would rock the ton and be so immense and shameful that his family would likely wish he had died instead. *But how do I live without her? And perhaps Antony too?*

Lina smiled and shifted so she straddled him, wrapping around him again. She sat in his lap, her legs and arms around his torso. "You know I can't do that, though I appreciate the heart with which such an offer was made. We will work something out, I'm sure. I will not let you go, but I cannot leave my girls either."

Benedict frowned. *Lina wanted to continue to be a brothel owner?*

"You don't need to continue running this place, Lina. I can keep you comfortable."

She laughed, the sound surprisingly harsh and cruel as she jumped off him. Her clothes appeared as though by magic and wrapped around her, covering her beautiful nakedness. Her supernatural speed was truly amazing.

He was relieved in a way that she was no longer naked. When she was covered it was easier to concentrate, but he longed for her naked body too.

"I don't need you to take care of me, Benedict. I have been doing this for a *very* long time now. I do this so that I can take care of the girls under my care, otherwise they would be out on the street. And it is an honest profession, despite your hypocritical society's viewpoint. Prostitution has been around as long as humans have lived on this Earth, so don't pretend you can give me better. I am safe and I am happy."

Benedict moved to his feet, lightheaded, and dizzy. He gathered his clothes and frowned as he began to dress. Her anger and opinion didn't make any sense. "I thought you would want to be out of this profession, Lina."

She scowled at him.

Benedict blinked. *What did I say wrong?*

"You have no idea what these women have been through or who they are, Benedict. So, do not assume to judge them. Or me."

He pulled his jacket on and tucked his cravat into his pocket. *How had this conversation detoured so much?* One moment he had been proposing marriage, a lifelong commitment, and the next they were fighting over her brothel. *How preposterous.*

"I don't—"

She stomped her foot, a veritable dark princess in this strange off-beat conversation.

"You do! Your society is *full* of these stupid rules. Gentlemen may fuck who they like, especially whores. When you are single, when you are married, it doesn't make a difference. You may treat women like slaves, then call yourself a gentleman."

Benedict frowned, anger growing in the pit of his stomach like smoldering coal. He'd never treated women like that. He'd had a permanent mistress that he treated very well, though he intended to pay her out, as he didn't need her anymore.

"I wasn't judging your girls," he said in earnest, trying to placate her. "I just thought you may like to stop working and let me take care of you."

Lina was truly angry now, steam practically fuming from her ears.

What was wrong with her?

She flew to the stairs and began stomping up them, muttering to herself.

"You have no idea. I *want* you to take care of me for eternity, Benedict. I want you to be right there with me. And all you can think about is a damn house and societal marriage?"

Benedict stopped at the base of the stairs, his heart pounding. A sick feeling of inadequacy threatened to make him retch.

She was right.

He was only thinking about the now, and the next few years. But in a hundred years, what would they do for money? Where would they live? How would they stay safe? Did he even *want* to live forever? He had so much to figure out. And he had so many questions.

Benedict forced his heavy legs to move and staggered up the stairs behind her.

She had reached the landing and had already opened the door.

People bustled around. Beautiful women, young women, old women. Everywhere.

"Lina, I need your help—" A beautiful young girl came running up, then stopped when she saw him.

"I'm sorry, my lord. I did not realize Lina had company."

He automatically bowed to the young woman, obviously born a lady. Her aristocratic nose, her ramrod straight back, and pale white skin were the most telling signs.

"It's no bother. I was just heading home," He turned to his Domme, his vampire, his future. "Two weeks, my lady?" He quirked an eyebrow and waited for her to calm down. He could almost see her struggle not to pick him up and throw him across the room. His lips kicked up at the thought.

"You can come every night, Benedict, you know I would see you." Her eyes softened as she spoke, and Benedict realized her feelings for him were deepening. She no longer saw him as *just* a food source.

"I have several things I need to sort out. I will return in two weeks." He bowed to her, confused but slightly amused at the same time.

Her eyes were flashing mutiny, and her lips were turned down in a frown. Lina opened her mouth to object, then seemed to think better of it and stopped.

Benedict turned away, and then realized he was no longer in his society anymore, not really. He had no rules to follow. Lina had elevated him above it all, time was no longer a barrier. He turned back in an instant and pressed his vampire beauty into the wall with his body, claiming her lips with all the passion in his soul. He used his tongue to pry her lips open and groaned when she relented.

She pressed into him in return and wrapped her arms around him, squeezing tight.

He pulled back, his breath coming out in pants.

Her eyes were glazed over and her lips red and swollen from his kisses.

"Goodbye, my lady," he breathed.

She nodded.

So, he turned on his heel and walked away, knowing that he had to put his old life to rest before he could start anew.

TWELVE

"What are you trying to do to us, Benedict?" Mother sobbed, weeping into her kerchief. "Destroy every small creature comfort we poor older folk have left?"

His father stood over her, shaking his head in dismay and disappointment.

Benedict ran his hand down his face, his head throbbing with a monotonous rhythm. It seemed there was no way to get through to them! "I have spent the past week trying to explain this to you both," he said, his temper flaring. "You have spent *all* the money you have and most of the money you were likely to make in the next *ten* years!"

His father flushed, in anger or embarrassment.

Benedict wasn't sure and he honestly no longer cared.

"We assumed you would fix everything once you inherited," said his father.

"Fix it?" Benedict leaned forward in his chair and glared at his parents. "If you mean, you thought I would marry some poor woman who had enough money to make our lives bearable, again, then you don't know your son very well at all."

His parents shared a long look, one that said they were completely blindsided.

His mother's tears disappeared as quickly as they had arrived, proving her emotions to be treacherous and false. "What do you mean, Benedict?"

He sighed again, giving his parents his harshest stare. Talking to his parents really was like trying to reason with toddlers. He might as well be arguing with a wall for all the good it seemed to do. "I mean, I am disappearing to Europe shortly, to gain an occupation. I will be gone for a long time. I have sold some shares of mine and have rented out two of the country properties."

His parents inhaled sharply, clearly devastated that their four homes wouldn't all be available for a visit at any time. They certainly wouldn't miss him when he was gone, Benedict was sure.

"I will give you both a strict budget and I will put money into the accounts to ensure the debt is paid off. If all goes to plan, then no matter how long you live, you won't run out of finance. But you *must* live within your means. I cannot support you and myself completely, not with the way you've been burning money like it grows on trees."

His mother burst into tears. She was only sorry for herself.

Meanwhile, his father glared at him, his rose-colored cheeks reddening further.

"I leave tomorrow," Benedict said firmly. "So, please let me know if you have any further questions before then." Benedict moved to the door.

Both of his parents ignored him, too devastated that their easy lives and flippant way of existing had finally come to an end..

The elderly butler stepped forward. "Can I do anything for you, my lord?"

Benedict turned to him with a smile. "No, I thank you though, Reynolds. You have been a wonderful friend to me over the years. Please keep an eye on these two for me and send me a letter if they get into any real trouble."

The butler nodded and bowed. "I will do, my lord. Safe journeys to you."

Benedict went to bed early, his head still spinning with numbers and problems. He wouldn't be missed by his parents, which was horrible really. He was their only son, and his parents honestly didn't seem to mind that he was leaving forever. And he had only a few gentlemen friends that might care, but they weren't really close enough to him to worry.

With his will finalized, and his family's finances organized, he was free of his responsibilities; but still unsure about what he wanted to do in regard to his entanglement with Lina. Yes, he wanted her, and he certainly couldn't be with her forever if he wasn't turned... but what would it truly mean to be immortal?

THIRTEEN

Benedict had been dozing lightly when a creak to his right caused him to sit bolt upright. Fear raced through his veins as his heart pounded and sweat broke out on his brow.

The old man from his strange visions stood in front of him.

He swallowed nervously.

The vampire smiled knowingly. His fear must have been palpable to one with such heightened senses. "You know who I am?" The vampire's voice was deep, and rough, as though it had been used too much or not enough.

Benedict released the blankets he had clutched to his chest and relaxed his hands. "You are Lina's maker," he answered.

The vampire bowed and moved closer.

Benedict slipped out of bed, unable to stay seated. "I am Benedict," he introduced himself and waited.

"You could not pronounce my real name, so you may call me Sil."

Benedict nodded, watching the careful way the other man moved. "Sil." Speaking the vampire's name caused him to shiver, a strange déjà vu feeling settling in his gut as though he had already lived through this moment somehow.

"You know why I have come?"

Benedict shook his head in the negative. "I hope you haven't come to turn me. I am not ready yet."

The old vampire chuckled. "No, Benedict, I have not. Lina will want to change you herself; I am sure."

Benedict frowned, his fears dissipating. *Then this makes no sense.* "Then why are you here?"

Sil walked up to him and inhaled through his nose, his ancient fangs extending down over his lower lip for a moment, before retracting just as quickly.

Benedict forced himself to remain perfectly still even though his instincts screamed at him to run. His palms were sweating, and his breathing turned ragged.

"I am simply curious as to who Lina had chosen."

Benedict shivered again. Sil's blue eyes were as deep as an ocean. Would such a vampire be jealous? Benedict knew Sil and Lina had been intimate, though the thought turned his stomach. "She told me I wasn't a choice. She said we were destined or fated."

The old vampire laughed again, looking pleased. He moved away toward the fire and sat in one of the chairs there.

Benedict followed, choosing the opposite seat.

"There are blood bonds between humans and vampires. These bonds mean that we are compatible mates. It doesn't mean anything else. Lina will crave your blood and your body as she has never wanted anyone else before. That is all."

Benedict flushed in surprise. *How candid a summary.* He swallowed down the nerves threatening to overpower him because he needed to ask something else. "But is it possible to have a blood bond with more than just one vampire?"

Sil's eyes widened, and he moved forward on his chair, the wrinkles in his skin creasing with the emotions flickering on his face. "I have heard that it's possible, though it is extremely rare."

Benedict nodded. He had thought as much. Antony's memories were coming back to him in his dreams, often more vivid than Lina's.

Sil raised an eyebrow. "Why do you ask?"

Benedict was of two minds about what to do. He didn't want to tell Sil what he suspected but this may be the only time he might be able to ask an impartial person of such vast knowledge the question. "I saw both of their memories while they fed."

A whistle left Sil's throat as he appeared to be having trouble breathing. "Antony's also?"

Benedict shrugged, trying for nonchalance, though he was desperate to hear what the ancient vampire thought. "Lina dismissed it, but his memories are getting stronger." He stopped then, not wanting to share with anyone how strongly he felt about the two vampires who had only recently entered his life. He was still struggling with coming to grips with the intensity of it all, himself.

"Antony has been lonely for a very long time."

Benedict nodded but waited for Sil to continue.

"You will only see the memories of a vampire you have a blood bond with. Lina feeding at the same time could not influence such a thing."

Benedict's shoulders dropped in relief. He had thought himself mad.

The old vampire got up to leave, evidently done with their conversation.

But Benedict wasn't ready for him to leave yet. "Sil, may I ask you a question?"

Turning back, Sil nodded.

"I do not want to become a vampire yet, and I also do not wish for Lina or Antony to feed on others," he said, feeling strangely possessive.

Sil turned fully now, his green eyes burning into Benedict's. "That was not a question."

Benedict nodded, that was true. "I don't need to be turned, do I? If I am, they can no longer feed on me, can they?" Benedict was astounded by how casual he was being. Literally talking life and death, soul mates, and blood feeding. What had happened to his boring existence as a *ton* gentleman? It might as well have flown out the window!

"If you are not turned, you will die as all humans do and you will leave two very passionate, grieving immortals behind," said Sil.

The picture Sil painted was a grim one. Yet, he had years to decide what he wanted to do. *Decades really.* "And the sustenance they need?" he pressed.

Sil began walking, pulling back the curtains so that he could go out the window, on the third floor. "Vampires may feed off each other for a short time, but they will need a human in short order."

Benedict nodded, exactly what he had thought. "Thank you, Sil."

The vampire nodded once and was gone.

"SIL, I NEED HELP." Antony moved toward Lina's maker, an Original vampire. He would answer Antony's questions, surely.

"I know why you are here, Antony. There is no need to explain, my child."

His lungs burning, Antony gasped and collapsed into a chair to Sil's right. "How could you know what I seek, Sil?"

The ancient, but eternal youthful vampire smiled.. "I visited Benedict tonight and he spoke to me of you."

Antony's shock and pleasure overwhelmed him in an instant. He sat speechless for several moments, questions clouding his mind. "What did he say?" he asked anxiously, unable to hide his desire.

Sil smiled wider this time, his fangs extending slowly in remembered pleasure. "That he believes you are also his blood bonded mate."

A tight band squeezed around Antony's chest and for a moment he found it hard to breathe. "Is it even possible? I want it to be, but... Sil, help me. Can it be true?" Antony begged. He needed help. He felt completely lost. This was all unfamiliar territory for him, despite his age and experience as a vampire.

Sil raised his hand and stroked Antony's cheek, his touch cold and strange.

"You don't need my help, young one. I have witnessed your pain, watched your beautiful soul suffer because of your loss. It is time to let go."

Antony felt a tear well up in his eye, his first in a century. The pain in his body, so long buried, was swelling and overflowing the box where he'd hidden the blackness that stained his soul for so long. "But I can't just let Malcolm go."

"You won't be. He will be in your heart and memories forever. But you cannot continue like this—merely existing. If the fates in all their wisdom have designed another mate for you, you should not turn your back. Not again."

Antony hung his head, swallowing the pain leaching his strength. He had never admitted this to anyone, but now was the time.

"Malcolm never saw my memories when I fed on him, Sil. I loved him and his blood was the sweetest thing I had ever tasted." *Until Benedict's...* Antony silently finished in his own head.

"Then he was not your blood mate, my boy."

Antony hung his head again. He didn't want to hear that. For so long he had wanted to destroy himself, lost in the pain and regrets of what should have been. "I did not believe the old stories. I thought one or two of the signs would be enough. I thought what I felt was enough, that it was real."

Sil put his fingers under Antony's chin, lifting his head so that they were eye level again. Sil's green eyes were very dark, with flecks of pale throughout. They were beautiful and seemed all knowing.

"Young one, what you felt was real. You no doubt loved Malcom, but those stories are all true, full, and complete. You can and will have one blood mate who will conquer your heart and soul. They will see your memories and their blood will be the sweetest you have ever tasted. That is the way." His eyes were kind as he stroked Antony's cheek once more. "If you have truly found your blood mate Antony, then you need to embrace him. Such gifts do not come often in life."

Antony sat straighter in his chair, years of pain, isolation and desperation rolling off him. He closed his eyes as the tears flowed down his cheeks.

Sil's heavy hand landed on his shoulder and gripped hard. "Make sure he is indeed your mate, and then bond with him. It is the only way."

Antony nodded. It seemed he had no choice in the matter, not if he was ever to be happy again.

FOURTEEN

Benedict took a deep breath and stepped into the darkness, taking just one step at a time. He held the stone wall and counted, drawing in a breath with every step. Ten steps from the bottom, he came into the flickering light provided by candles scattered around the dungeon.

"You have come back, my pet."

At the sound of Lina's voice, he smiled, and goose bumps prickled over his skin. He had missed that beautiful tone—the thrill her voice gave him. "Yes." His foot landed on solid ground, and he opened his arms wide.

She flew into them without a heartbeat's hesitation.

Her sweet scent filled his nostrils, her cool flesh perfect in his arms. He grabbed her rounded ass and pulled her hard against him, groaning as his cock stirred. "I have missed you," he said, whispering the words into her ear.

Lina shivered with desire. "I have missed you also." She snuggled into him.

He smiled again. It was an amazing feeling to be able to just stand still, breathing with her, simply being with her.

"Have you decided what you want to do, Benedict?" Lina's voice broke into his trance.

His eyes sprung open. *How am I going to explain to her what I want?* "Let's sit down," he suggested, before he led her over to where the old chairs once were. "When did you acquire a bed?" He indicated the huge, ornate sleigh bed that was now a key point of interest in the room.

Lina shrugged and sat down on it.

Benedict sat next to her, pleased to find the mattress firm and comfortable.

"I usually rest during the day on the floor," she said. "But I wanted somewhere comfortable for you to sleep. For *us* to sleep."

Her gesture did not go unnoticed or unappreciated. His heart beat faster and his hope that she would allow him to remain human intensified. "Thank you, Lina. That was thoughtful. It's beautiful."

She smiled and stroked the back of his hand with her smooth nails. "Have you said goodbye to your old life, Benedict? Or have you come here to tell me you do not want me?"

The panic her last words evoked was instant and painful. Benedict laid a hand on his belly, trying to quell the feeling. Well, that certainly answered any lingering doubts he had. *I can't leave her.* "I have arranged everything as best I can, though I have questions."

Lina laughed in good humor and threw her leg over his waist, straddling him. Her hands came up to cup his face, her skin cool, needing his blood. "Of course, you do! And I will answer anything you wish to know. I just need to know that you have chosen me."

Benedict smiled and softly kissed Lina's perfect pink lips. "I have, though I would like to see Antony, also." Benedict held his breath.

Lina stiffened in his arms.

This may be a problem for her. But it isn't nonnegotiable.

"Antony? Why?"

Benedict stroked Lina's back and kissed her softly again. How could he explain to her that he wanted both of them? That he *needed* both of them? He couldn't sate one blood bond and ignore another… "I have been dreaming more of his memories, Lina, and I would like to see him again."

Lina's eyes widened. She cocked her head, leapt off his lap and landed on the floor again with feline grace. She turned her head back again, raising an eyebrow at him. "Your wish is granted, my love. Antony is already here."

Benedict turned in the direction of the stairs.

The muscular, dark-eyed male vampire was already standing at their base. The solid door and fifty-seven steps were no challenge to Antony.

His presence was calming, despite the hostility rolling off him presently. Benedict could still feel Antony's presence inside his blood. He saw his visions. And after Sil had confirmed Benedict's suspicions, he knew they were all linked—not just he and Lina.

Antony nodded his head in their direction, his black eyes heated yet wary. "Benedict, Lina."

Benedict smiled and nodded back, his heart beating an excited rhythm.

"Lina, I spoke to an Elder and they think I should explore my connection to Benedict."

Benedict's stomach dropped. *Did that mean the Antony just wanted to have sex with them again?* Benedict wanted so much more than just that.

Lina frowned and moved around him so that she partly shielded him. "I know what you mean by 'explore' Antony, and I won't allow you to feed on him again."

Benedict peered over Lina's shoulder and watched.

Antony's mood changed instantly, his eyes pleading as he held up his hands to Lina. "I know *you* think he only saw my memories because we were sharing him at the time. But I need to make sure. I have to know the truth of it."

Benedict opened his mouth to breathe easier as he realized what the gloriously sculpted vampire was asking for. Antony wanted to know if they were truly blood bonded too. *Thank God for that.* He had dreamed about Antony last night, had dreamed of fucking him. Seeing him in the flesh now set off every memory, every lustful thought. He had missed him, almost as much as he'd missed Lina.

"Antony, he is *not* your mate. I won't have you feeding on him just because you want to."

Benedict gaped at her. Lina knew how he felt about Antony, so why wasn't she allowing him access?

"I don't mind." Benedict stepped up close to them before Lina could protest again. He wanted this too. He needed to know why he felt more complete having both of them inside his blood.

Lina inhaled and hissed in surprise.

Benedict was sure that she could tell how aroused he was, how much he wanted Antony. Benedict wasn't ashamed of it, not anymore. He wasn't waiting five hundred years to feel complete. He couldn't believe Antony had. "I want to know too. I have missed you, Antony." He looked straight at the eternally beautiful vampire and walked toward him, tilting his neck ever so slightly. His heart was beating so hard that he felt almost sick with the pressure of it.

Antony's eyes widened, then he stepped forward, pressed Benedict up against the wall and bit into his neck without any warning.

Benedict gasped at the brutality. At how Antony's need to get the test over and done with was almost degrading. Memories flooded Benedict's mind, just as he knew they would. It was erotic and a deeply emotional thing for him. Antony was not savoring the connection, which was upsetting and pushed him to act.

Benedict grabbed Antony by the ass and pulled him in tight, forcing the vampire to feel him properly.

Antony removed his fangs from Benedict's neck, blood on his lips.

Benedict rubbed his hardening cock against Antony's.

Antony met his gaze, his dark eyes wide and fearful.

Benedict didn't know if Antony was more afraid that Benedict would see something, or he wouldn't. Well, Benedict had something to ensure power now and he wasn't giving it up easily.

"What did you see?" he asked anxiously, his heart in his throat.

Benedict smiled rather smugly. He wanted something first. "I'll let you know after I've fucked you."

Antony disappeared across the room, landing to crouch against the cross in the corner.

Benedict felt cold, and he wanted the weight of Antony's body back in his arms.

"You saw something more. Tell me now," demanded the male vampire.

Benedict glanced at Lina.

She who was observing the scene with a knowing look.

Benedict turned back to his male mate. He shook his head no. "After I fuck you, I'll tell you." Benedict looked to Lina for permission.

She was already half undressed. "Don't think you're leaving me out of this." Her remaining clothes disappeared, and she stood in the middle of the room, stroking her rosy nipples with her fingertips.

Benedict laughed, exhilarated, he was about to get everything he ever wanted. "You are our center, Lina. Why would we leave you out?"

She smiled, then pointed to the stone floor. "Both of you get naked and kneel before me."

Benedict looked at Antony, his lover's eyes still wild. Benedict began to undress. He was kneeling before Lina, cock outstretched for only one moment before Antony joined them, his naked body quivering beside him.

Lina moved over to Antony and lifted his chin up with a fingertip. "He won't hurt you, Antony. He can't. You know you are going to love it."

Antony shook harder, his eyes closed under the weight of his feelings.

Benedict couldn't imagine what it must feel like, to know your mates were finally within your grasp, after centuries of loneliness, emptiness, and guilt at having given up on someone you loved. To believe you may have found that connection again would be enough to shake the very foundations of anyone's world.

"I have never done this, Lina. Never been the... receiver."

She chuckled, knowing as they all did just how much Antony truly wanted what was being offered, if only he would surrender himself to their control. Lina turned Antony's head toward Benedict. "Kiss him."

Benedict turned his whole body toward Antony and waited.

The male vampire's eyes were huge pools of fear warring with desire.

Benedict spoke first. He had to. "Decision time, lover."

He lifted his hand and cradled the vampire's jaw in his palm, watching tears well in Antony's beautiful midnight dark eyes.

Antony shuffled closer and pressed his cool lips against Benedict's.

Benedict inhaled sharply at the surge of lust that one touch of Antony's lips released within him and wrapped his arms around the exquisite vampire's muscled shoulders. Pulling Antony's chest into contact with his was blissful. He needed the feel of Antony's skin against his, craved the strength, and yearned for the connection. And Antony gave it all to him, making him moan and cling harder.

"Enough." Lina's command was enough to break them apart, their Domme in dungeon.

"You are both ready, but I am not. I want you to work on me, bring me to the brink, but do not penetrate me until I give you permission."

Antony stood and lifted Lina up into his arms, walking across to the new sleigh bed. *Their* bed. Antony placed Lina in the center of the mattress and lay down on one side of her.

Benedict took the time to simply gaze at them side by side, soaking in their beauty before he chose to take his place by their woman. Benedict stared at Antony for another moment, then bent his head to kiss Lina's neck. Sucking the skin into his mouth, he bit down slightly.

She shivered in response and ran a hand down his back.

Benedict moved his lips down to her breast. He licked at the abundant flesh before homing in on the nipple, breathing hot air across it, before sucking hard.

Lina shivered again.

Benedict looked up to see Antony giving her other breast similar attention. His balls tightened in anticipation. He wanted to claim the other male—needed to know how good it would feel to *own* him.

Benedict began moving down, kissing each inch of Lina's taut, creamy flesh until he found her wet core. She was ready for them, more than ready, but she had asked for more and he wasn't going to disappoint her.

He glanced up.

Antony was artfully using his hands and mouth to tease and torment Lina's breasts.

Benedict turned his attention back to her pussy. Holding her fleshy thighs open, he licked her from ass to clit.

Moaning, she quivered as her legs tried to clamp together.

Benedict knew he was no match for her vampiric strength, and if she had truly wanted to close her legs she would have. He smiled to himself as he sucked her clit into his mouth.

She screamed, arching her back. Her taste was like rich honey, her cool skin reddening as she became more aroused.

"Stop, I want you now."

Benedict moved to his knees and looked down at the two vampires, both of whom were stronger than him, both of whom he wanted more than anything else in this world. "Antony, on your back." He pointed to the mattress and avoided Lina's gaze. He couldn't order her, but he needed to get this position right.

Antony moved over to him slowly, his eyebrows rising in question.

Benedict moved back off the high bed and stood, gesturing to the handsome vampire. Excitement raced through his veins and his cock throbbed in anticipation of what was to come.

"Lie on your back and lift your knees. I want your ass here." Benedict patted the space on the mattress directly in front of his cock.

Antony looked up at him, fear and excitement warring in those dark depths.

Lina stepped in. "Do as he says, Antony. Benedict, please get some of that oil for yourself." She pointed to an elegant glass bottle by the bed.

Benedict moved over to the table and grabbed it, poured some into his palm and then stroked himself with the lubricant. *Fuck*, the wet heat felt so good, and he continued to prime himself, moving his hand up and down.

Antony moved into the position Benedict had requested, his muscular thighs quivering slightly as they opened.

Benedict took a moment to admire the submissive position and the trust it displayed. His heart ached; he was so honored. He returned with the bottle and positioned himself between the male vampire's strong legs. Applying more oil to his fingers, he gently eased them inside Antony's ass while staring down at the beautiful vampire.

Antony hissed and arched his back, fighting the strange mixture of pleasure and pain.

Benedict remembered how it felt when Lina had done it to him. It had increased his pleasure by at least double.

Lina expertly swung her leg over Antony's body and raised herself up over his stiff cock. "Look at me, Antony."

He must have looked, but Benedict couldn't see anything except Antony's thick cock disappearing within Lina's pussy.

She impaled herself completely, crying out in ecstasy when she was fully seated over him. "Take him, Benedict, take him now," she instructed.

Benedict lined the head of his cock up with Antony's tight ass and pushed in, past the tight ring of muscle that tried to force him out and pressed deeper into his mate's body.

Antony groaned, his knees moving together in response.

Lina pushed them further apart. She leaned back, her spine pressing up against Benedict's chest as she began to ride Antony like the seasoned professional she was.

Benedict stepped even closer and wrapped his arms around Lina while thrusting into Antony, his hot flesh engulfing him. He didn't want to wait, and he couldn't take it slowly. Something was riding him hard, a need to claim, and a want to give pleasure. Being with these people was the most intense, fulfilling moment of his life.

"You are both mine." Benedict growled the words and thrust harder into Antony's tight body. He would never last inside Antony, he felt *too* good. He needed to tell his lover. "Antony, I love how you feel. I'm going to come so soon." Benedict snapped his hips faster, enjoying his mate's moans of pleasure as he thrust deeper. "You are so tight and hot. Tell me that you feel me."

Antony grunted, his body bowing up and his legs beginning to shake. "Your cock feels so good, Benedict. Please don't stop," he begged.

Relieved and almost out of his mind with pleasure, Benedict put his hands around Antony's hips and moved harder, faster, and deeper. He pummeled Antony with everything he had.

Lina began to tremble and screamed as she hit her peak. "Benedict..."

He lifted a wrist to her mouth and groaned as she bit into him. Pain skewered through his mounting pleasure.

Antony thrust up into Lina, his ass squeezing tight around Benedict's hungry cock as his vampiric seed pumped inside her.

Benedict leaned forward, holding his hand as far as he could reach out to his male.

Antony's sharp teeth bit into the flesh just below his thumb, spilling his blood.

Benedict moved once more, furiously burying himself to the hilt inside his mate, his seed exploding out of him in a volcanic torrent to join the three of them together—forever.

FIFTEEN

Antony's heart was about to explode. He had never been taken in such a way. It felt like his soul had been stripped bare, and then rebuilt even stronger.

Benedict withdrew from his body.

He winced. *That will take some getting used to.*

His human mate moved onto the bed, lying beside Antony and putting an arm across his chest, holding him close. The gesture was sweet, endearing, and loving. No one had ever touched him in such a way, not in all his long years.

Antony's heart swelled anew, but the caution that came with heartbreak and age told him to check before he committed himself too fully. He turned his head and asked the question that would secure or destroy his future happiness. "Tell me what you saw."

Benedict tilted his head up and kissed him on the lips, the gesture again gentle, and loving. Then he laid his head down on Antony's shoulder and cuddled in like he intended to stay there forever. "I saw you making love to a black-haired, blue-eyed woman. I think she must have been your maker."

Antony's body began to tremble uncontrollably, the moment even more shocking than he had anticipated. *I've found my mate, my true blood mate!* He could be whole again.

Lina moved down onto Antony's other side, cradling his head to her beautiful bare breast. "It's all right my love. It's all right," she whispered to him as his life changed forever.

Benedict gripped him harder.

Antony shook with sobs as red tears poured down his face. He didn't even try to control them or stop the flow. He needed the release too much. He needed to be free of the burden he'd been carrying to make way for this new paradise his heart had found.

Minutes passed and his tears dried up, the emptiness inside him slowly filling up with light. The rest of his life awaited him, what were they waiting for? He turned toward Benedict and wrapped an arm around his human. "Benedict, we will turn you as soon as possible."

Antony began kissing his new mate, along his jawline and down his throat. Now that his quest for confirmation had been achieved, his arousal was flooding him all over again. Benedict smelled divine. He always did, his blood and scent were custom made for him and Lina. But his scent mixed with the smell of sex and cum was absolutely intoxicating.

He let his hand stray to Benedict's hip and moved across to the now soft flesh. This man had a beautiful cock, thick and a perfect length. Antony's ass was a little sore, but he would swear that even after five hundred years, his last orgasm had been his best ever. The emotional release afterward had only sweetened and enhanced his surreal pleasure. The tears had been cathartic to his tortured soul.

"I don't want to be turned yet, Antony," said Benedict gently.

Antony froze and looked up. He couldn't have heard what he thought he had. "Pardon?"

Benedict rolled away from him with a sigh and got off the bed. He walked across the room to his breeches and pulled them on.

Antony missed his nakedness instantly and clenched his hands into fists to stop himself from reaching across the room and stripping Benedict once again. When they were all vampires, they would lock themselves into a room and stay naked forever. Someone would bring them a human to eat on occasion, but it would no longer dominate Antony's thoughts. He had two people to pleasure forever now.

"I know you both want me to stay with you forever. And I will, I want to. But I don't wish to become a vampire just yet," Benedict explained.

No! Antony released an animal-like growl and flew *at* his mate. Blind with anger and fear, he extended his fangs, gripped his Benedict about the waist and connected with his neck—hard. He felt a moment's regret at his sheer level of brutality as Benedict groaned. But Antony continued to feed, past caring as Benedict's sweet blood flooded his body like a tidal wave of sinful joy. He would turn his mate now and damn the consequences.

He felt Lina move, her fear and anger flowing over him.

She was screaming at him.

But he couldn't stop, this was *too* important. Not just for him, but for the three of them. He couldn't let Benedict grow old or get injured before he was turned!

Benedict reached up and threaded his fingers through Antony's hair.

The gentle touch made Antony moan as he feasted on the most delicious blood of his life. Even Malcolm's didn't compare.

"Antony if you force this on me... I won't stay mated to you..."

True fear ripped through him as Benedict's words registered. *God, no.* That would be worse than dying again. It took all his strength, but he pulled his fangs out just before the point of no return and stepped back, horrified at what he'd done.

Benedict started to slide to the floor.

Antony reached out and caught his cold body against him. A wave of guilt he hadn't felt the like of in a hundred years beat down on him. He swung Benedict up into his arms and placed him gently back on the bed.

Lina flew into place, cradling Benedict in her lap like he was the sacred and perfect treasure on Earth, something to be savored and protected at all costs.

"How could you do that, Antony? You bastard! If I hadn't been scared that you'd kill him, I would have ripped your throat out!"

Antony moaned as Lina's pain assaulted him. Her anger and fear were as real as his. He could feel how much she wished to hurt him and punish him for what he had just done. And that made his own pain *so* much worse. It felt tangible, like a hot blade in his heart.

Benedict began to stir.

Lina stroked his hair again.

Antony knew he needed to fix what he had done. He needed to apologize. He moved forward wanting to touch them.

Lina wrapped her arms around their mate and growled at him, a feral nasty sound that he truthfully deserved.

Antony stepped back in terror as the full weight of his actions settled on him. *What have I done?*

"Lina... I'm all right." Benedict started struggling to sit up.

Lina helped him, propping him up a little when he would have fallen back.

Pain sliced across Antony's chest as he realized how close to death's door he'd brought his mate.

Benedict's normal health and natural sense of vitality were gone. He was pale, his eyes almost devoid of all color and warmth. He looked terrible.

"It will take you a few days to regain your strength, but I'll look after you until then," Lina reassured their mate. You're going to be fine; I promise."

Benedict nodded while he took a deep breath. His eyes were unfocused, then they sharpened, looking directly at Antony.

He should be doing what Lina was doing, reassuring Benedict. Antony stepped a little closer, meeting Benedict's gaze. "We'll both look after you."

Another feral growl ripped out of Lina's throat in response to his declaration.

Antony fell back again. *I need to make this better, but how? How do you make up for almost killing the person you love?*

"Lina, stop. I want Antony too," whispered Benedict.

Lina looked ready to murder one of her oldest friends.

The reality of his actions finally settled in Antony's head. He had betrayed his mate. "It's not all right, Benedict. I'm sorry." His voice was thick with emotion, but he forced himself to continue. A part of him registered that Lina was no longer angry at him, but his own grief was drowning him now. Everything hurt. His head, his chest, even his legs felt weak and boneless.

"I should never have done…" His voice broke off again as he moved closer to the bed. What if Benedict didn't forgive him? And left them both forever? Lina would never forgive him. And he couldn't bear to be apart from Benedict, now.

"It's fine Antony… I know…" said Benedict, his voice raspy and weak.

Antony shook his head and collapsed to his knees in front of them, tears pouring down his face. He had lost Malcolm because of his own stupidity. And yet Fate had blessed him over a hundred years later with his *real* mate and he had betrayed him.

"You don't know… you can't possibly…" He had to make Benedict understand, beg his forgiveness. But the pain was too much, and he was sobbing now. His head too heavy to hold up, he let it sink to the floor as his whole body hunched over in pain. He would do anything, *anything* to have Benedict's forgiveness. He felt a cool body slip down beside him.

Benedict pulled Antony into his arms.

His head lay against Benedict's weakened heart and the sound just made his pain worse somehow. *Because it's my fault.* "You don't… you don't… I just feared and—" He sobbed and clung to Benedict's form.

Rocking him like a baby, Benedict whispered, "Shhh, my lover, shhh."

Antony kept crying, unable to stop. The pain was just so bad. His soul was being torn from his body, or at least it felt like it. He tried again to explain. "I need you, we both need you. I can't lose you! If you die..."

Benedict laughed weakly at him, the sound reassuring in a strange way. "I'm not going anywhere, Antony. I want you both, too."

He didn't understand. It didn't make sense. "I'll kill myself if I lose you too, Benedict. I'll walk into the sun... I just can't do this anymore, live half a life..." Antony knew he wouldn't survive losing Benedict like he lost Malcolm. He truly would rather die than live another single day with a huge gaping hole in his chest.

Lina wrapped her arms around him and gripped him hard, showing him that she was there to support him too. Then she inhaled sharply and spoke, her commanding Domme voice, breaking through his depression. "Antony, listen to me. Benedict wants you. He's not leaving us. Do you understand?"

Antony's sobbing decreased as soon as he heard Lina, the command in her voice the anchor he needed to pull himself out of his pit of despair. He nodded his head but squeezed his eyes tighter shut.

"You are to stop this right now. You are losing all the blood you just took from our mate."

Antony forced his blood drenched eyes open and looked up at Lina.

Lina flew across the room and came back with a square of material. She wiped the blood from his face and bare chest. Her touch was soothing, further numbing the pain. "Listen to me. What you did was wrong, but Benedict understands why you acted the way you did, and he forgives you. But, now we must both listen to him."

Nodding, Antony forced himself to sit up. She was right. Lina, his tiny female mate, picked him up and put him on the bed, then came back and did the same for their suffering human mate.

Benedict sat propped up against the rounded backboard, looking horribly weak and pale. He raised a hand, wrapped it around Antony's neck and guided him onto his thigh.

Antony went willingly, the happiness returning to his heart like the moon appearing in the dark night sky as his cheek nestled into Benedict's leg.

Lina sat opposite them, smiling.

He felt her contentedness, her pride. They were both hers now.

"Tell us, Benedict. Explain to us why you do not wish to become immortal." Antony closed his eyes, too exhausted to say anything more.

Benedict's voice was weak and strained. "I will become a vampire one day. I know I have to, at some stage, to stay with you both. However, I need to be human for a few more years."

Antony stroked along Benedict's long legs, his eyes opening again to watch his hand. What beautiful skin his mate had.

Lina asked the first question. "Because you want to maintain your place in society?"

A small smile crept onto Antony's face when he heard Lina grind her teeth together. She was frustrated with the situation and with Benedict. He understood the feeling all too well.

They would have to pay a human to watch Benedict through the day if he was determined to stay mortal. They had to make sure he stayed safe… and alive when they couldn't be with him.

"I'm sure we could manage a few years of that. Couldn't we, Antony?" she asked when Benedict didn't answer immediately. Lina stared at him expectantly.

Antony closed his eyes tight, nodding his head against Benedict's leg. He would do anything to keep his mate.

Benedict laughed gently again. "I don't care about society, and I don't want to go back to my old life. Though, I think we should move out of London, to make it easier for my parents. They need to grow up, in a manner of speaking."

Antony sat up, confused. "Then why would you want to stay human?" He cleared his throat, the sound strained and clogged full of unshed tears. He'd never felt like such a wreck. Not since *he* was a human!

Benedict looked down and ran his finger along Antony's thigh.

Antony shivered, the touch unexpected and beautiful. Benedict really did love him.

"Because I don't want you feeding from anyone else."

Antony's head flicked to Lina.

They shared a shocked glance, before returning their attention to their mate.

"We can feed from each other as vampires, Benedict," said Lina.

Benedict shook his head and moved his hand closer to Antony's swelling cock.

How could my body possibly respond like this after the night I've experienced?

"I know you need a human and you both love my blood, above all others. Correct?" Benedict continued.

Antony and Lina shared another glance. This was dangerous territory.

Lina spoke up this time. "Benedict, that is just sustenance, the food that keeps us alive. We will do *anything* to keep you with us forever, including turning you tonight and never tasting your human blood again. Any sacrifice would be worth keeping you safe."

Antony nodded emphatically. He couldn't have said it better himself.

Benedict set his jaw, stubborn as the day was long. "No. I want to be the one to feed you. Not forever—but for now."

Antony couldn't believe all this had been over Benedict wanting to please them. He was thoughtful, considerate, and generous. Tears welled in his eyes again. He had betrayed the soul who wanted nothing more than to please him. "Benedict... I..."

His lover silenced him by leaning forward and kissing him softly on the lips. His cool skin was a reminder of how much blood Antony had taken.

Two tears slipped down his cheeks.

Benedict pulled back. "Enough, Antony. I understand why you did what you did, but no more," he said sternly.

Antony swallowed and nodded, unable to speak while he regained control over himself. It wasn't easy. His throat ached with the need to scream out.

Benedict swayed slightly. "I'm tired, my loves. I need to sleep."

Antony looked at Lina for direction.

She smiled. "The sun will be up soon, so we may as well rest too."

Antony watched as Benedict curled onto his side.

Lina rolled into his chest, snuggling up.

"Here Lina?" Antony asked cautiously. He knew he looked ridiculous sitting up in bed, looking down on them. But he hadn't slept beside someone in over a hundred years.

Lina's eyes were already closed, her expression peaceful. "I got the bigger bed for a reason, Antony. Lie down," she said softly, all traces of anger and judgement gone.

Bemused by her forethought, he lay down and spooned into Benedict's back. With a sigh he laid his arm across his two mates and an unexpected electric shock shot right through him. He groaned and kissed the back of Benedict's neck in gratitude and relief.

I am whole.

Lina moaned and gasped. "Did you feel that, Antony?" she whispered as Benedict dozed off.

Smiling, Antony closed his eyes. "Yes, my love. I think it means we're meant to be. We'll never lose him now."

EPILOGUE

Three years later.

Lina's belly tightened in an expected way as she watched her beautiful mates together.

Antony was unbuttoning Benedict's shirt slowly, kissing the skin as he revealed the muscles beneath, heedless of their audience. Antony was anxious and being overprotective.

She knew that he wanted everything to go perfectly. He wanted nothing but the best for the man who filled the hole in him that had been left empty for so long.

Their human mate was breathtaking, everyone thought so. They had been offered money, power, and other humans in exchange for him.

Lina smiled to herself as she remembered the sizable chunk of flesh Antony had ripped out of the last vampire to suggest they share Benedict with others. She would never have believed such happiness could possibly exist as they had found together.

Despite his mortal status, Antony and she enjoyed every moment of loving Benedict. He had given them so much. His love, his devotion, and his sweet blood every day. They didn't feed fully from him, but he always offered while they made love, which was so often it sustained them and meant all the more.

Thus, both Antony and Lina never needed to feed from anyone else and Benedict was happy. Their unique relationship had survived despite all the naysayers. In fact, they had flourished—all three of them. It was like an impossible dream come true.

"Please come forth," said Sil as he held up his arms and beckoned.

Lina and Antony stepped forward and flanked Benedict's now naked body. A ring of vampires old and new surrounded them. A few laughed, a few looked envious, but mostly Lina saw only happiness from them. Finding your blood mate above was a rare and precious thing; and most vampires recognized that above all else.

"We have been waiting for this moment for many years." Sil looked out over the brethren of vampires, and they quieted down. "Many of us did not think such a union could work, but it did, and still to this moment does. As a result, Benedict's gift to his mates has been long debated as well as envied."

A grumble of assent surrounded them.

Lina looked over at Antony, a smile trembling on her lips.

His dark eyes lit up as his mouth pulled into a smug smile.

Benedict had exclusively fed them and had never once been interested in sharing anything with another vampire—sex or blood. The sort of love and loyalty he gave them on a daily basis was the main reason they had never pushed for this moment. They had waited for him to be ready.

"Join hands and speak the vows you have chosen," said Sil.

Lina, Antony, and Benedict turned their bodies, so they stood in a triangle, a hand clasped with each of their mates.

Two bloody tears trickled down Antony's face.

Lina leaned forward to lick them away.

He smiled apologetically, but Lina saw the tears that trembled on

Benedict's lashes also. Her two strong men. She nodded at Antony to go first.

"Lina, I have loved you for centuries and tonight we will make our bond official. Benedict, you do me the greatest of honors for allowing me to turn you, but also for joining us for eternity in this mating. I love you."

Tears tracked down Benedict's face.

Lina leaned forward to lick them away. His tears were always so salty. She licked her lips and nodded to her human. It was Benedict's turn.

"Antony, Lina, I love you both. More than I thought anyone could possibly love anyone. I will always do anything for you and tonight I will prove that. If my human life is the price I have to pay to be with you both forever, then I pay it gladly."

Lina squeezed his hand, nervous for the first time in centuries. It was her turn. She cleared her throat and spoke loudly, proudly. "Three years ago, I didn't believe in blood bonds. How could I have a mate in the world looking for me and I for him? Then Fate sent you to me, Benedict. I will never be more grateful for that than I am at this exact moment in time. You complete Antony and I, join us, and fulfill us. I pledge my undying devotion, protection, and love to you, for as long as I exist."

Antony squeezed her hand.

She looked at both of her men, wanting to kiss them, and take them into her body. But now wasn't the time.

"You are joined, Antony, Lina, and Benedict." Sil's voice boomed over their small congregation. "Turn Benedict this night and he will be forever yours."

Lina let go of Antony's hand but kept a hold of Benedict's. She and Antony had discussed this, and they both wanted to turn him. It would take precision, but they could do it—if they were careful.

Antony glanced at her.

She nodded. It was time.

Benedict leaned forward and kissed her lips. Then he turned his head and kissed Antony also. It was a gentle but surprising gesture. "I'm ready." Benedict closed his eyes.

Lina took a deep breath, nodding again to Antony.

They extended their fangs and Lina bit into the side of Benedict's throat.

At the very same time, Antony bit into the other.

They held their mate to them tightly, supporting him as they drained his delicious blood from his veins.

They moaned as one, in pleasure and agony. This was the last real time they would ever drink from him for their sustenance, their life force. His blood was the most decadent, delicious thing for them, especially during the height of orgasm. To no longer have that would be hard, but what they were gaining together was so much more valuable.

Lina groaned and drank more, warmth and pleasure spreading through her body in tangible, pulsating waves.

As they felt Benedict's heart slow to the point of stopping, they broke away and ripped at their wrists with their own fangs.

Lina moved her wrist over Benedict's mouth.

Antony lined his up also.

As their blood flowed into Benedict's mouth, he gasped and gurgled, some spewing out the sides of his lips while more still poured down his throat. His skin pale and clammy as he tried to swallow, and it was horrible to watch.

She had never turned anyone before, and the fear began to mount. Lina looked over at Sil for confirmation that they were doing the right thing.

Smiling, he nodded.

A pile of cushions had been arranged earlier for Benedict's comfort. When he actively swallowed no more, she picked their mate up and carried him over, placing him in the center.

Benedict lay deathly still for moments, looking as fragile as a flower—here for a season, then gone.

Lina clutched Antony's warm hand in her own, her chest so tight she was afraid she would expire. "He looks like he did three years ago," she whispered.

Antony nodded, two more tears of Benedict's bright red human blood slid down his cheeks. It had taken Benedict weeks to recover from Antony's attack, but they had built a fortress out of the ashes. And they would do so again.

"Sil, he's not moving." Lina's voice began to tremble as her fear overcame her strength.

Antony's arms came around her as her chest became a burning mass of pain. If they lost him, neither she nor Antony would survive it. She would sooner die before experiencing the loneliness of losing her mate.

Sil flew to their side and placed a hand on Benedict's chest. Smiling, he turned Benedict's head slowly.

Lina watched in amazement as their bite marks glowed red against his skin.

Benedict's eyelids began to flutter.

Lina fell to her knees beside him.

Antony was only seconds behind her. Antony sobbed as he clung to one side of Benedict and Lina to the other.

"Are we consummating our marriage already?" he asked.

Benedict's voice, now deeper and sleepy, was the sweetest sound Lina had ever heard. She pushed herself up, threw her leg over his warm body, and straddled him. Her cheeky human was now her magnificent vampire. "Not yet my love, but soon." She leaned down and kissed him, tasting his newly immortal lips, grateful beyond measure that he had survived the process.

Benedict looked at Antony who now lay on his side with his head propped up, and then back at her, his green eyes blazing. "Are we bonded now?"

Antony leaned forward and kissed Benedict.

Lina threaded her fingers through her men's hair, binding them to each other and to her. "Yes," she whispered, closing her eyes and sending up a prayer of thanks to the heavens. *"Forever."*

* THE END *
Read on....

~

MARIE'S STORY

~

Ten years ago—when I wrote this story as my first ever Menage romance—I had several critique partners reading my work as I improved my craft and learned new things every day about writing.

One of my critique partners asked me to write Marie's story. She said that I couldn't just leave Marie in the brothel... So, I wrote this super steamy extra short story to give sweet Marie the happily ever after she deserved!

~

CHAPTER

ONE

London 1816

I lifted my hand and knocked on the door to Lina's private room. The one that led downstairs, far beneath the building. I didn't truly understand why she went down there during the day, nor did I care to be honest. Lina had saved me and protected me, when others would have used me far more poorly and abused me without a second thought.

But I had to get her up. The customers had started to arrive, and the women of the brothel needed Lina to make sure everyone followed the rules. When long minutes passed and there was still no answer, I tried the handle hesitantly. When it turned, I took a deep breath and opened the door reluctantly. "Lina, I'm sorry to disturb you but we need you in the front room," I whispered down the dark stairwell,

There was a time when that sentence alone would have brought Lina up the stairs faster than you could take your next breath, but since Lina had found her mates, things had changed.

I strained my ears and heard sounds of lovemaking coming from the room fifty-seven steps down. Despite my occupation, hearing

Lina's honest moans of pleasure and her mates enjoying each other was enough to flush my cheeks with heat. I couldn't interrupt them now. *I can handle the new clients tonight.*

I closed the door and straightened my dress as I entered the main sitting room and smiled at the six gentlemen standing and waiting for service in the center of the foyer. "Good evening, sirs. Please speak to whichever lady you fancy, and she will take you to her room. If you have any questions, please feel free to come and speak to me."

Four of the men moved immediately to one particular woman, who smiled and left with them.

I held my head high and circled the room. My heart was hammering in my chest with tension and anxiety, but I didn't want anyone to know I wasn't confident in this new role. I'd never worked a night without Lina's supernaturally strong presence.

A high-pitched cry sounded from a room down the hall.

I jerked my head towards Mason, our guard.

He nodded and set off at a run.

I sighed and went to stand at the head of the room once more. Such occurrences were an occupational hazard, unfortunately. Some of the men who paid for whores like us were rough—more than rough—occasionally. A few of the women, like me, could handle a little more than others. We'd had three new girls start with us in the past month alone and not all of them were settling in very well.

"Well, if it isn't the Mistress' favorite little lady." The nasty voice and threatening tone belonged to one man.

Lord Somerton. I clenched my hands into fists within the folds of my skirts, remembering far too well the last time this man had been in the brothel. He'd found me alone in my room and tried to force himself on me. Only Lina's speed and strength had saved me from being forcibly taken that night, but he'd left me with injuries, nonetheless. I raised my chin and stared him straight in the eye, anger overcoming fear. "I believe Lina asked you *not* to return."

He leered at me, his gaze lingering over my covered body.

Something about his sour, leering demeanor made me shudder with disgust.

"She did... but Lina isn't here right now, is she?"

A tremble of fear passed over me, but I refused to give in to the feeling. I bit down on my lip to stop any whimpering sounds from escaping. I could handle this by myself. *I can.*

The older, clearly intoxicated man stepped closer and grabbed my arm. He squeezed tightly.

I gasped as he hauled me against his soft body. "Lina *is* here! She's just downstairs! So, you better go before she sees you." Pain flickered in my flesh as I struggled against his hold.

He held my arm tighter, then twisted.

My heart thumped erratically, my instincts screaming at me to run, but I literally couldn't.

"You're mine," he whispered as he bent forward and licked my face in the most obscene gesture of ownership.

I cried out as I arched away, trying desperately to break free.

He only grabbed me about the waist and hauled me closer again.

The fear of this nightmare finally coming true had my legs shaking so strongly, I dropped against my captor's body. *No, please no!*

He moaned and pressed his hardened cock against my hip. The already dim light within the parlor faded as I swooned with fear. It would be over soon...

"Release the girl. Now."

The unknown voice had me crawling back into consciousness as my abuser relaxed his grip on me and turned towards the voice.

I managed to twist around so that I could look up at my savior, a man with long, flowing white hair and serene green eyes.

Lord Somerton released me in an instant.

I fell forward onto my knees.

"Ugh!" I put my hands out to the carpeted floor and took a deep breath to calm my nerves.

The newcomer, who was now in control of the situation, placed an arm around me and lifted me up.

I was soon standing upright again, at his side. I swayed on my feet and pressed into his strong body, grateful beyond belief that he had chosen to step in when he did.

The man stiffened as I touched his side.

When I looked up, I saw long, white fangs extending down across his bottom lip. *He's a vampire.* Like Lina and Antony, of course! I needed to protect him from discovery. I tried to step a little away from him.

His hand stayed on my waist like he couldn't bear to let me go.

The pressure of his touch gave me the confidence to do what needed to be done. I lifted my arm and pointed to the front door, feeling strong and protected. "If you leave now, I won't tell Madame Lina you dared to show your face here, again."

Lord Somerton glared at me for a moment, then slunk away, leaving the premises, angry, embarrassed, and unfulfilled.

I turned to the handsome vampire, tears of gratitude springing to my eyes as curiosity stirred in my mind.

He had turned his head away while I dealt with the other man, but when he looked back at me now, his fangs were still extended.

I knew what Lina was, had cleaned her room often enough to know perhaps too much about her... And I was absolutely fascinated. "Would you like to choose someone also, sir?"

The vampire assessed me, his deep green eyes flickering over my face.

I focused on the white gleam of his fangs, enraptured by my unexpected hero.

"Yes. You," he said.

I swallowed and bobbed a curtsey in acceptance of his request, anticipation making my stomach tighten and flip. "Yes, sir. I just need to wait for Lina to arrive and then I can take you to my room. I can't leave the floor unattended."

He frowned. "Where is she?"

I smiled as the heat rose to my cheeks again. I should be over such silly responses but being born a lady... it was a hard habit to break. Or so it would seem. "In her room with Antony and Lord Benedict."

The vampire closed his eyes and spoke Lina's name in a low, drawn-out breath.

My own breath caught in my throat at hearing the deep, husky tones of his voice. He was older than I, that was for sure, but there was something about his demeanor that made him seem ancient. Powerful. *How old could he be?*

Not two moments after the vampire called her, Lina walked into the room looking much unlike her usually perfectly polished self. Her dark brown hair was disheveled, and her gown was not yet laced up, but she was at least covered. "Maker, you have *very* bad timing."

The vampire tilted his head towards me but didn't apologize for disturbing Lina.

Maker? He's Lina's maker?

"I want her, and she said you must come attended the floor first."

Shock didn't quite describe the look on Lina's face. She looked between me and the vampire who'd made her. "And Marie is agreeable to this?"

I nodded quickly. Lina was very protective of me, for which I was very grateful. Lina had taken me in when I'd been thrown out of my parents' home and would otherwise have starved on the streets. Lina never gave me to anyone whom she believed to be dangerous. She was very much like a mother hen or a big sister.

However, as I gazed upon the vampire who had protected me this night, lust and gratitude beat through me with the strength and force of ocean waves during a storm at sea.

Lina's eyes widened again, as though shocked by the fact I wanted to be with someone so powerful... so... majestic. But Lina didn't say anything else, she simply smiled and began to tidy her appearance.

My stomach tightened and I swallowed the strange squeak that threatened to rise in my throat. *This was it. I'm going with him!*

CHAPTER

TWO

I indicated the stairs and turned to walk that way, my heart still thumping in my chest. "This way please, sir." My voice trembled as I spoke, and my breath hitched in my throat. I had to calm myself, or I'd swoon on the steps. So, I took careful, measured breaths and picked up my skirts, my heart beating harder and faster as I ascended each step up to the second floor.

I pushed open the door to my bedroom, then moved closer to the bed and turned back to the entrance.

The silent vampire had followed me into the room, and he closed the door.

A thrill shot through me that I couldn't even identify. It made the hairs on my arms stand on end and my nipples tighten with a thrill beneath my corset.

The vampire sat, fully clothed, on the chair against the wall. "You may call me Sil," he offered.

A shiver vibrated down my spine at the sound of his voice. It was so deep, so ruggedly beautiful. I loosened my dress and smiled at him. An action I'd done so many times before, yet tonight felt special, different somehow. *And it is different*, I realized. Tonight, would be the first time

I'd be going to bed with a man purely based on my own choice. *This is happening because I want it to.*

"I am Marie." My body heated in foreign ways, responding to my need to please the man in front of me. The place between my legs ached, throbbing with more need than I could ever remember having felt. I glanced across the room at the bottle of oil next to my bed. It stopped me from being damaged when my body was unprepared for doing my job. It was a helpful hint I'd been given on my very first night here. But perhaps this would be the only night I wouldn't have to use it?

I dropped my dress and pushed it to the floor, now standing in only my pretty chemise and bloomers. "How would you like me, sir?" I asked.

Sil smiled at me, his eyes lighting up with pleasure. His fangs had retracted, and he looked to the world, like any other man. "Marie, I have no wish to force sex upon you, but I would like to feed on you, if you will allow me?"

My belly fluttered wildly in anticipation of sharing this with Sil, while a deeper part of me filled with disappointment. He didn't want me as a man did? I scolded myself for being disappointed, and focused on what he *did* want.

Lina and Benedict's relationship had intrigued me from the first moment I realized they were together. I knew Lina fed from Benedict. He often floated about the house, looking like a man who was drunk, but didn't smell of liquor. He was on some kind of constant and blissful post-feeding high.

When I'd seen that look on Benedict's face, it had inspired a yearning in me. Now, I had the chance to experience it for myself. "Yes, Sil, I would love that. How would you like me to... Shall I sit? Or...?"

Sil indicated to his lap and sat a little straighter in the chair. "Sit across my lap, Marie. If you will."

I saw him inhale deeply as I moved closer, as though scenting me. His fangs extended again in a way that made me hurry to get into his lap. I loved that he had chosen me to feed upon and I didn't want him changing his mind. I lifted my legs and stepped over his thighs, slowly straddling him, but keeping my pelvis away from his and resting my hands on his cool, hard chest.

I wasn't sure which he'd prefer, so I decided to ask. "Wrist or neck, Sil?"

Sil wrapped his strong hands around my hips and pulled me closer to his body until my thighs opened to accommodate his hips.

I gasped at the sexual move and watched his full lips move closer to me.

He tilted his head. "Neck, please." His calm voice and slow movements were at odds with the hardness swelling between my legs. He leaned closer.

I arched my back so that I could press my breasts against his chest, exposing my neck. A heartbeat later and I felt a sharp pinch in the flesh of my neck, and I let my eyes close. Then... the most amazing rush of pleasure came over me as my blood flowed out of my body and into his.

Flashes of people penetrated my mind as he fed on me.

I saw Sil standing with Lina... then another woman with beautiful blue eyes, then the scene changed, and I saw a young man with almost black skin. Sil's incredible body naked, bent over them. Covering them. Loving them. The constant reel of pictures, like memories, was incredible. I never wanted it to stop.

Sil moaned as he fed on me.

It was the most lustful sound I'd ever heard. It caused my nipples to peak beneath my dress and my body to ache for him. I couldn't stop myself from responding to the feelings flowing through me, so I began to move. Rolling my hips and rubbing my now wet body against his hard cock.

Sil broke off from my neck and ran his smooth, hot tongue over the wounds.

The feeling was healing and sweet. "That was amazing, Sil..." I managed to say, though my head swam and for the first time in my life, I felt completely wanton. *And wanted.*

He continued to moan against my neck in a way that had me gasping with need. "Marie... you have the sweetest blood..."

His strong hands came up to cup my breasts through the thin material covering them, his thumbs sweeping over my nipples.

Tingles of pleasure speared through me, making me ache and throb for a deeper possession. I moaned with abandon, rocking my hips faster against him. Heat sweeping down my legs and rippling through my belly.

"God... I want you..." moaned Sil, his voice a breathy, strained whisper.

Then I was suddenly laying on my back, on my bed. Alone.

Sil had fled.

I covered my mouth with my hand to stifle the sob that rose, but I stayed where I was. On my cold, hard mattress, where he'd deposited me. I slipped a hand down my body and lifted my skirts, feeling between my legs to investigate my body's response to Sil. Slippery lips and sticky inner thighs greeted my fingers and I had to swallow the moan that rose within me.

I ached with unfulfilled need and my mind reeled with pictures of Sil. I wrapped my arms around my body and squeezed my eyes shut tightly to stop the tears that wanted to spill. I just couldn't forget this had happened. Especially not when Sil's reaction to me was surely as strong as mine was to him.

My life had been forever ruined by a cruel nobleman three years ago, when he'd foreclosed on our home and forced my parents into poverty. Lina had taken me in, given me a job and kept me safe. But I wanted so much more out of life, than just *this* existence. And somehow, it felt like Sil could be connected to that dream of 'more'...

THREE

Sil's presence here tonight had breathed to life a flame inside of me, a burning I had thought long since dead and extinguished. Heedless of my near-naked state, I got up from my lonely bed and ran down the stairs to find Lina.

Antony was kissing her softly near the empty entrance way since most of the girls were now engaged with clients.

"Lina, I'm sorry... please... Antony..." I babbled and gasped for air. I shouldn't have run so fast. I hopped from foot to foot in my excitement and apprehension and tried to slow the racing of my heart.

The two pale vampires turned to me, their pleasure-glazed eyes clearing when they saw me.

"Marie, what's wrong? Where's Sil?"

I gasped from the stitch in my side. I'd *definitely* run too fast down the stairs.

"He— he bit me, and I *saw* things and we were... and then he left!" Tears sprang to my eyes as I felt the loss of him once more. I wrapped my arms around my body, trying to stay warm.

Lina and Antony took a deep breath, probably smelling my arousal. I blushed hotly, my cheeks burning with blood. But I would not be deterred. I couldn't lose the one person who made me feel like I was more than a mere ghost of who I'd once been. "Would you take me to him, please?" *Surely, they'd know where Sil lives?*

Lina and Antony exchanged glances.

For a breathless moment I feared they wouldn't.

But then Antony took off his coat and wrapped it around my shoulders. "I will," he offered, the perfect gentleman vampire.

I gasped as Antony swung me up into his arms, still barefoot. Lina's lover shouldn't be holding me like this, it made me uncomfortable. I made a strangled noise in response and struggled in his arms.

Antony held me tighter. "It will be much faster if I carry you."

That made sense, I supposed, since I didn't know where Sil lived. It could be anywhere. And I could never hope to keep up with Antony's supernatural speed. I forced myself to calm down and tentatively put my arms around Antony's neck.

Lina reached out and touched my arm with a gentle hand, then stroked my cheek slowly. Her eyes were filled with love.

I smiled at my long-time protector.

A red tear slid down Lina's cheek. "Go to him, my girl, and be happy. I have a feeling you won't be coming back."

Nervous excitement beat hard in my chest. "Thank you for everything, Lina. Will I ever see you again?'

My Madame simply smiled and reached across to stroke Antony's cheek tenderly. "I love you. Please take care of her."

Antony leaned into Lina's hand for a moment and then we were outside and moving fast.

The wind whipped by my face and my eyes were unable to keep up with how quickly we were moving. I closed my eyes and held on tightly to Antony's muscled arms until we suddenly stopped.

"Open your eyes, little one."

I heard Antony's voice and did his bidding, though part of me was terrified to see where he'd brought me so quickly. Had we *flown* there?

We were inside a dark room, but I didn't know *where.* The air around me was warm, fed by a glowing fire in a grate.

Antony set me on my feet.

I turned towards the sound of Sil's deep voice.

"You should not have come."

My stomach dropped in disappointment, but I moved closer. I wasn't turning back now. He could keep me as a feeding tool if he wished. I wasn't going back to the brothel. My eyes adjusted slowly to the dim light, seeing the only man I'd ever wanted, seated upon a large chair.

"I'm not a child, Sil. Please don't send me away again."

Antony stepped up next to me, bowed deeply before Sil as though he were the King himself, then disappeared, leaving us alone.

I unclipped Antony's jacket and allowed it to fall to the floor.

Sil moaned as though he were in pain and shifted in his chair. "I am over a thousand years old, Marie. You don't know what you are asking."

I haven't asked anything yet. But I knew one thing. I wanted him. In whatever capacity he would have me. Any life with Sil was better than one as a whore. I unbuttoned my chemise, then let it drop to the floor. My nipples were tightening, despite the warmth of the air. "I know I want you," I said as calmly and boldly as I was able.

I swallowed hard, the emotions buffeting my system, too intense to be able to speak easily. I didn't know if it was from him feeding on me, or the pure attraction shared between us, but I didn't want to go on without him. I just knew I couldn't... "I beg of you, please don't send me away. I could stay with you and let you feed from me. That is... if you don't want all of me. But I'd be happy with anything you would offer." I gestured to my body and looked down at the ground, embarrassed. If he didn't want me in the same way I desired him, I'd understand. *Or... I'd try to!*

Sil's gentle fingers lifted my face up, though I hadn't heard him move. "Of course, I want you, Marie. That isn't why I need you to leave."

I threw my arms around his neck, pressing my now half naked body against him.

His arms were strong and bulging with muscles. His chest was chiseled, and his body was as hard as mine was soft.

I looked up into those gentle green eyes. "Please, don't stop yourself if you feel the same way I do. I need to feel this for more than one moment in time. When you fed on me, and I saw those pictures in my mind... I loved it so much. I want to see it all again. Feel it all again. My body wants you as it's never wanted anyone before. *Please.*"

Sil put his hands under my bottom and lifted me up against him.

I wrapped my legs around his slim waist and held on tight.

Then we were sitting back in his chair and my head was dizzy again. It would take a long time to get used to the speed with which vampires moved.

"What did you just say?" he asked quietly.

I gasped loudly as I pressed my aching pussy against the hard swelling between his legs and began to move against him. "Sil, I want you." I cupped my own breasts, my nipples pebbling tightly.

Sil looked down at my nipples, his cool, capable hands coming up to brush my hands away to stroke the skin with his own fingers.

I arched my back, pushing the flesh into his palms eagerly. "Oh, please, Sil. Please." I'd never wanted to feel a man inside of me. And I hadn't known the satisfaction that could come from the one you want stroking a place that ached so much. *But I do now...*

Sil dropped his head and put his hands around my waist, pulling me up to him and sucking one of my nipples into his mouth.

Pleasure arrowed down between my legs, and I threaded my fingers into Sil's lovely, long white hair, holding him to me. I didn't want to let go, in case he tried to disappear again.

Sil ripped my bloomers off my body with one flick of his hand.

I was completely naked and it wasn't enough. "Touch me, please," I begged, my body writhing with need.

FOUR

S il chuckled at my impatience.

But I didn't care how wanton I sounded. My pussy tangibly throbbed for him. I'd never needed anything more in my life than to know the pleasure felt when a man and woman joined like this, willingly, and with such need and passion.

Sil flicked his thumb over my swollen clit.

I yelped out at the foreign feeling, writhing in his lap. I forced my eyes open and looked down at Sil's lips. His fangs were extended but that wasn't what I wanted to feel just yet. I wanted a kiss. I pulled his face up to mine and pressed my lips to Sil's, reveling in what was essentially my first real kiss. Not a kiss forced or taken, but a kiss *given* in desire.

As he pressed my lips open and slipped his tongue inside my mouth, he pushed a long finger deep inside me.

Something inside me shattered at that moment. I moaned and convulsed, digging my nails into his shoulders as my body exploded in a kaleidoscope of pleasure.

"I shouldn't, Marie..."

I heard Sil's words against my ear and moved my hands down to free his straining cock from his breeches. I couldn't understand why this was such a bad idea for him, but at that moment, I didn't care. Reasonably, being with me couldn't be any worse than being alone for a thousand years!

Determined to have everything he had to offer and to give everything I had in return, I raised myself up.

Sil removed his hand from between my legs to grip my waist tightly.

I shifted my pelvis until I felt the large head of his cock nudge my wet outer lips. *Yes!* I smiled as I pressed down, embracing Sil in the most intimate way. The slide of Sil's cock forged a new passage within me—no oil needed. I moaned loudly as I shifted to accommodate him. He was large, but I kept bearing down until I enveloped him completely.

Sil gasped and threw back his head, gripping my hips harder. "Marie, you feel like heaven…"

I put my hands on his shoulders and began to move, rocking my hips and building speed as I slid up and down his hard shaft. I listened to the pleasure thrumming through my own body as well as the sounds of his pleasure and tried to move in the best way I knew how. I rode him like it was all that mattered. Like this might be the only time we were bonded this way—I had to give it my everything.

The wave of rapture within my belly built again, the heat roiling through my blood with a mind of its own. "Oh my God, Sil!" I panted and gasped for air, each slide of his cock within my body stoking the fire of our desire higher. Finally, when my belly was as tight as a coiled spring and I didn't think I could take a single second more, I threw my head back and let go, allowing the storm to take me. I cried out as raw, unbridled euphoria crashed over me like a wave.

Sil grabbed my hips with both hands and began thrusting into me hard and fast, pumping and moaning with his own intoxication until I imploded once again. At the perfect moment, he bit into my neck and his seed pulsed into me with hot, all-consuming spurts of bliss.

I shuddered and moaned as I clung to his neck for dear life. "Oh…

God..." Flashes of images, more vivid than the last, passed through my mind. Of Sil when he was younger, and when Sil was still a human... amazing colors and feelings assaulted me, imprinting on my mind forever.

Too soon, it seemed, he drew back from my throat.

But it was enough. *More than enough.* I smiled down at him and bent my head to kiss glorious lips once more. They were warm now. Meanwhile, sweat dotted my skin with the supernatural exertion of it all. "Thank you," I whispered against his soft lips, never more grateful for another being in my life.

Still inside me, Sil reached up to caress my flushed cheek with his hand. "Tell me what you meant when you said you saw pictures when I fed on you."

I smiled dreamily, my eyes sliding shut. I nestled my head onto his shoulder and sighed happily. "The first time I saw you with Lina and two other people, but this time I saw you as a younger man—I think when you were still a human. I just love you feeding on me. The pictures are my favorite part. Well... also the amazing bliss I feel."

I was beginning to drift off to sleep but Sil's shaking shoulders brought me quickly back to reality. I opened my eyes and lifted my head, devastated to see blood red tears sliding down Sil's pale skin. *What have I done?* "Sil, did I say something wrong?"

He shook his head, his hands stroking down my naked back reassuringly. "Not at all, Marie," he answered. "The truth is I'd given up finding you hundreds of years ago. I thought I'd missed out on my chance for a blood mate."

I stroked Sil's face, wiping away the tears that had finally stopped flowing. I didn't understand what he was talking about, and why was it something to be so upset about? "A blood mate?" I asked.

He leaned forward to kiss me tenderly before pulling back to explain. "A blood mate is a person predestined to be your life partner, as Benedict was for Lina and Antony. Your mate's blood is the sweetest thing you'll ever taste and you know them when they see your memories as you feed on them."

My relief at this explanation was so acute, tears welled and slid down my cheeks. "So you won't get rid of me?" I shuddered with a deep sense of overwhelming relief.

Sil chuckled and tightened his hold on me. "Never. We will be bonded and then I will turn you. We will be together forever, fair Marie."

If that was what he was offering, I didn't want to wait. "Turn me now. Please." I tilted my head and leaned closer. I could live forever, with him! Always wanted. Always protected. Always special. I literally couldn't ask for anything more.

Sil frowned at me for a moment, then looked longingly at my neck. "I usually perform the mating ritual myself, as I am among the oldest in our community, and there are usually witnesses present."

I glanced up at him. Desperate now. Despite what he said, I didn't want him changing his mind. "Please don't wait. We don't need anyone else, do we?"

He appeared to think about it for a moment, then nodded. "As an officiant, I believe my brethren will trust in my authority. First, I will speak some words and then you may also say something if you wish. Then I will turn you into my immortal lover."

"Yes, please!" I practically squealed as I waited impatiently on his lap.

Sil took a deep breath, then began. "Marie, after a thousand years, Fate has sent me the one person designed for me. My feelings are hard to express. Ecstasy, joy, relief. I will spend the rest of our existence looking after you and loving you. For all time."

My eyes welled with unexpected tears once again and I bit my lip in an attempt to stay them. I suddenly realized what this mating ceremony really was. What it truly meant. I was *marrying* Sil. *More* than marrying him. I was committing to love him and stay with him for eternity. I should have felt overwhelmed, but all I could do was rush into my own vows, lest he change his mind.

"Sil, I knew the moment you saved me that you were special. When you touched me, I wanted you as I have wanted no other. Being with you feels right, like it's exactly what's meant to be. Please turn me now, so I can stay by your side and love you forever in return."

One more red tear slid down Sil's cheek as he exposed his long, white fangs. "Not long to wait, lover." And he bit me.

I closed my eyes and held him to me. He drank and drank far past any other time, my life leaching out of me and into him with every beat of my heart. As the darkness grew inside my body, I welcomed it, knowing Sil would find me on the other side of death—and only then would my new life truly begin... An eternity with love and happiness... an eternity as an immortal with my very own blood mate.

THE END